The Faery Codex

The Faery Codex
by
Flora-Beth Edwards

The Faery Codex

ISBN 978- 1-908577-97-9

British Library Cataloguing in Publication Data.
A catalogue record for this book is available from the British Library.

1 3 5 4 2

Printed and bound in Great Britain by CPI Group (UK) Ltd.

Hawkwood Books 2020

CONTENTS

Dedicated to all those who still believe
in the magic of this world.

1. The Ancient Force

Ava burst into her bedroom, grabbed her rucksack from the floor, tipped it upside down and emptied everything on the bed. 'It must be clean and tidy before I start packing,' she told herself as she rummaged through the disposed contents.

A varied collection of sweet wrappers, chewing gum, plasters and train tickets filed through her hands. 'The plasters I'll keep, just in case.' Putting them to one side, she paused at the train ticket, fearing to pick it up then pinched it at the corner as she brought it closer to read.

Had it really only been two weeks since she arrived here?

Had it been just two weeks since her father's disappearance? And look what she had learned in that time! She had seen a world only witnessed by a chosen few.

She feared her destiny. She did not want this task but it was the only way to bring the Son of Prophecy back and free her father.

After throwing the sweet wrappers away, she held the train ticket tightly in her hand, closed her eyes and tossed it into the bin. It was a return ticket, but Ava knew she would never be returning home; too much had changed. She had changed. She was no longer the same girl who had arrived there two weeks earlier, lonely and afraid. There was something inside her, a power that had been switched on. She had a world to defend.

She stared at her empty rucksack. 'What do I put in it? What do I need? Where am I going? My journey is North but that is all I know.' Sighing, she flopped onto the bed and sat shaking her head. 'Dad help me, what do I need?'

A gentle breeze from the open window carried the scent of honeysuckle and elder blossom. It was sweet. She had known that smell before. Ava opened her eyes and reached for her notebook and pen. 'We always need to keep records, Dad. We need our journal, don't we?'

Grabbing her purse, she threw it in the rucksack alongside

plasters, a pen, and a field journal. That was all she had packed. Everything she really needed was inside *her*, not the bag. She was ready!

She was so different from that girl of two weeks ago. Two weeks from that night when it all began...

It was too late to be night and too early to be morning. Ava was in an in-between and this was their time.

There it was again, the screeching in the dark.

It sounded like an animal howling in pain and yet at the same time, undertones of mocking rippled through the air.

Ava pulled the quilt around her and scrunched her eyes tightly together. 'Please go away, just go away. Go away.' She whispered under her breath. 'Please go away.'

Again, the screech.

It wasn't a night owl but it was a sound that once heard you would never forget and it seemed closer that time. Ava pulled the quilt over her head and rolled herself into a ball. She closed herself off from whatever was out there, encased within her bed like a child in the womb.

She wanted the morning to come. She needed the daylight. Everything was better in the light. There was after all, nothing to fear in the daylight. The sun's warmth made the monsters of the dark disappear and melt away like the cold-hearted creatures they were.

This was all new to Ava, she didn't believe any of it. She had stayed with her Aunt Winifred before but now there seemed to be a permanence to it. Aunt Brenna and Aunt Fawn had showed Ava her bedroom with equal enthusiasm, pointing out how they all had a go at redecorating her 'grown-up' room, 'all' being the thirteen women that seemed to be at permanent residence in the house. Intermittently, they would be vacationing somewhere else, probably their own houses. Many of the women were not local either so they would come for rather long holidays.

"We thought you wouldn't want it pink with castles anymore," Aunt Brenna said.

"But we knew you would like all your things around you,"

Aunt Fawn added.

Fawn and Brenna were from Ireland and would come over for the summer to the house, Candlesby Manor. They had got married there a couple of years ago and Ava had been their flower girl. The house had been full then and yet there still seemed to be space.

The house was large, to say the least. It had over one hundred and eleven rooms. Granted, some of the rooms were no bigger than a broom closet whilst others were huge. The kitchens were the full length of the house and had been cordoned off into three. What house had three kitchens?

Yet the house itself was spectacular. Approaching it you would think you were going to a cathedral. It had tall steeple spires reaching for the sky and the central part once housed the clock tower. However, this room had been closed off for some years after Great Grandma Evelyn had ordered it locked. The clock tower had been struck by lightning in one of the worst storms of the century. The clock and the original tower had all been destroyed.

Ava had never been in the attic, let alone the new clock tower which had since been built. It was permanently locked, an empty room Ava had been told. Her father, Professor Riley George Fellow, also had never been in the room and neither had his sister, Winifred.

Ava wondered what her father and aunt had been like as children growing up in this huge house with its own library, three kitchens, one hundred and eleven rooms, church spires, and the most wonderful staircase to slide down ever imagined. Painted walls depicting ancient battle scenes adorned the hall, whilst banquet scenes greeted you in the dining room.

The house had an armoury and a billiard room though no-one ever played billiards. Ava thought it was just a posh name for snooker and what was the point of that? Waste of space, she thought, but then again, the house did have all those rooms. One could waste space in a house that size!

Ava's grandfather had built the house in 1735 and wanted it to be round, but it seemed to be growing in a giant snail shape that never ended. To the point that the house was like a maze

3

going around and around on different levels.

The clock tower was level seven, the attic level six, the nursery was level five, the bedrooms levels four and three, the drawing rooms level two, the library and dining room level one, and on the ground floor was the armoury, billiard room, ball room, morning room and conservatory. Finally, the basement with its three kitchens and wine cellar. All levels were connected by stairs and that magnificent staircase that you could slide down all the way from the clock tower to the basement.

Ava had never slid down it that far. The most she had ever done was three levels and that was enough. Thinking about it, her heart still pounded with fear.

'This is ridiculous!' Ava was angry with herself, as the screeching drew closer. She pulled back the quilt to breathe. She was boiling under it. 'It's outside you fool, and you're safe in here.' Reassuring herself she threw off the quilt completely and stretched out in her bed.

The screeching stopped and she turned to the window. 'Finally,' she mumbled before fluffing the pillow and lay staring at the ceiling in the darkness. As she closed her eyes she felt the room move. She stared at the ceiling and saw it shudder, stronger and stronger and stronger, vibrating so much that she thought it might collapse.

In the centre there formed a yellow-white mass accompanied by a humming sound, like a distant sonorous song. There was a flash and she felt heat for a moment. The glowing yellow-white mass appeared like a smokeless fire, growing on the ceiling.

Ava opened her mouth but no sound came out. She wanted to scream, she wanted help. She felt the air leave the room and it was difficult to breathe. In her mind, she wished for the light to turn on but she was paralysed and couldn't move.

'Please go away!' she wanted to shout, but they were not just words, they were powerful emotions. She projected all this onto the entity forming above her, every cell pulsating within, focusing her intent.

Her bedside light came on. 'Did I do that?' Ava asked herself as she tried to move her hand, but she was still paralysed

4

with fear. She stared at the ceiling and saw the yellow-white mass shrink smaller and smaller until it disappeared into a little pin hole of light.

She rolled herself tighter into a ball as the screech returned. It seemed to be outside her window. 'Please, please go away. Leave me alone. Dad, where are you?' she mumbled into the quilt as she started to feel weak, almost drained of energy. The gentle lull of nothingness encased her. As she drifted away into sleep, the screeching grew fainter and fainter until it was lost in the dark recesses of night.

2. Fairy Godmother?

A screech of car tyres upon the gravel awakened Ava. The fresh morning light spiralled its way through a tiny crack in the curtains which had not been drawn completely.

She preferred her curtains to be totally closed. They needed to be overlapping so no darkness could ever find its way in. The curtains became a solid wall keeping the night at bay, whilst she was safe behind it in her room.

The roar of Aunt Winifred's motorbike outside brought her back to reality. As she lay watching the sun's ray twist and turn through the curtains, particles of illuminated dust danced downwards to the floor.

'I suppose I should get up,' she said to herself before sighing and pulling the quilt back, scratching her head and ruffling her hair as she opened the curtains. A hive of activity could be seen in the courtyards. Several cars were parked alongside auntie's solar powered motorbike.

As she ventured down the stairs, the closer she got to the morning room which doubled as a conservatory. It was full of plants, mainly herbs which were now in flower. Approaching the morning room, she could see a group of 'aunties' all gathered round Winifred.

"I heard him again last night, Winnie. He is getting close."

"We have to protect Ava."

"I know. I know but…"

Ava sneezed. 'Damn herbs,' she mumbled under her breath.

All aunties turned to her.

"Good morning, darling. Sleep well?" Aunt Winifred took the lead while the others dispersed in various directions leaving only her and Lexi.

"Well, actually no."

"Oh dear!" exclaimed Winifred.

"I heard a weird noise."

"Weird?"

6

"Yes," replied Ava turning to Lexi. "Not quite an owl, but not quite a dog howling either. At one point I thought it was outside my window."

Lexi shot Winifred a look but before she could speak, the other said, "I'm sure it was nothing darling. We do live in the countryside after all and there's all manner of strange sounds out here compared to what you're used to."

"Well... there was something else..."

"Breakfast," Winifred said, holding up a basket full of chocolate bars.

"Chocolate for breakfast, auntie?"

"Of course, in this house, why not?"

Ava gave a little exasperated laugh. She knew there was no point in continuing with her 'strange noise' conversation, her aunt had changed the subject completely.

"Oh auntie, please never have children."

Winifred put the chocolate laden basket down and reaching out to Ava replied smiling, "Well, bless you for thinking I still could."

Lexi giggled at that and asked, "Hot chocolate Ava?"

"No thank you, but tea would be nice."

"Perfect, mint or chamomile?"

"Normal is fine."

"Normal tea?" Lexi asked, confused.

"It's alright Aunt Lexi, a glass of fresh orange juice would be lovely."

"Ugh! Now that I can do," replied Lexi as she wandered off to the kitchens leaving Ava staring at the chocolate basket.

"What do you normally have for breakfast then Ava?"

"We always have a cooked breakfast. Dad says it's the most important meal of the day."

"Cooked?" Winifred seemed puzzled.

"Yes, bacon, eggs, sausage, beans or scrambled eggs on toast or kippers or smoked mackerel. Dad always made sure we had a good hot breakfast, especially when we were out on a dig, as we would be so busy and researching we would lose track of time and sometimes skip lunch."

"You enjoyed being on dig sites with your father then?"

"Yes, they were the best of times, sleeping outside in tents, being close to the past. Scraping soil away and revealing a whole new world."

Winifred's voice was soft.

"You sound like him. He loved all things belonging to the past. He was always searching for something new. He believed in other worlds and was determined to find them. Until at last one found him."

"Auntie?"

Winifred composed herself and gave a little shudder.

"Oh, listen to me, I'm sure your father is well and he's just on some excavation site somewhere in the world and he's lost track of time."

"He's been missing for two weeks now but the police said there was no need to be concerned because of the note he left."

"Well, that's right. He just had to go and look at that Temple."

"But I don't believe it. Dad would never leave me. We went everywhere together."

"Maybe this time he did and just needed to be on his own."

"But it doesn't make sense, none of it does."

"Now Ava, you are so suspicious. Let's just enjoy the time we have together eh? I see so little of my only niece, with you gallivanting round the country with your father."

Winifred gave Ava a hug as Aunt Lexi returned with the orange juice and toast.

"Fresh orange juice, and I thought you might like toast. That's normal, isn't it? Toast is normal?"

"Yes, Aunt Lexi, it is."

Ava sat down at the table as Lexi placed her toast and fresh orange juice next to her while Winifred rummaged through the chocolate basket for her breakfast.

A welcome tap-tap-tap could be heard on the stone floor. Turning around, Ava beamed, "Jennifer!" as Jennifer's paws softly padded upon the cool floor.

"What? Oh yes, she is still with us. Perhaps, you'd like to take her for a walk later?"

"I'd love to Aunt Winifred," replied Ava, ruffling Jennifer's curly hair and ears.

Jennifer was Winifred's Welsh terrier. All four of her legs were a light tan but her back was black. She had the most beautiful face, all tan with two black ears. Her nose was long and brown and she was adorable. Her lovely curly coat was turning grey slightly and she hungered for cheese. She had the most exquisite big, brown eyes, the sort you would see on the cutest teddy bear.

After breakfast, Ava and Jennifer went for a walk on the estate. Ava needed some time to get away from the madness of the house, mainly to think about what had actually happened last night. She wanted desperately to tell Aunt Winifred but knew she would dismiss it.

Ava put Jennifer on the lead. She didn't have to, but when Jennifer was on the lead she thought she was going somewhere special, even if it was just round her own garden.

The grounds of Candlesby Manor were huge and consisted of woods, orchards, a lake and a swimming pool, which was near the house. Ava preferred the woods, something about the water made her nervous like it had a presence of its own.

Jennifer pulled on the lead as she and Ava neared the woods. The trees on the estate were hundreds of years old. There had been a forest here long before her distant grandfather had built the house, so perhaps the trees were even older than anyone thought.

The daisy lawn that surrounded Candlesby Manor was shaded by the great trees, but Ava soon left this behind. The honeysuckle and elder blossom filled the early morning air. As birds sang their songs of morning glory, sunbeams bounced from the leaves of trees that had witnessed the turning pages of history.

Lost in thoughts, Ava found herself alone and some distance from the house when Jennifer spotted something or someone and ran off towards the darkest part of the woods, yanking her lead from Ava's hand.

"Jennifer!" Ava called and ran after her. Picking up the lead, she wrapped it round her wrist and scolded, "Jennifer, really…"

The dog glanced up at Ava and sort of cowered.

"It's alright, I'm not…" Ava stopped and noticed her surroundings, frightfully dark, shaded by heavy leaves and ancient trees that reached so high Ava couldn't see the sky. The strange music she had heard the night before came again, and a fluctuating, swirling light from within one particular tree.

Jennifer yelped and took off again in the direction of the house, pulling Ava's arm until the lead snapped. Ava stood frozen to the spot. Just like last night, she couldn't move.

The smokeless void took form but she couldn't see any features in it, just a yellow-white glow surrounding it.

What was it?

What did it want?

Ava's thoughts swarmed round her head as she tried to speak until she heard a voice resonating from the glowing mass.

"I am the ancient force that gives you life… find me."

It wasn't a human voice, it had no compassion, no feeling whatsoever. It was the sonorous sound, an imposing deep and full sound made manifest into words.

The light faded and Ava's legs felt wobbly, like they were too weak to carry her. She fell to the ground as darkness encased her.

3. The Truth

A beam of light twisted its way through the crack in the curtains. Had this happened before? Ava rubbed the sleep out of her eyes and watched as it slowly turned, illuminating the dust in an early summer's morning. She felt groggy and tired, like her strength had been drained from her again. Realising this had all happened before, she pulled herself up in bed and placed a pillow behind to lean on.

A face peered round the door, tall, blond hair, with angular features and piercing blue eyes.

"Hello Tarran."

He turned around to call downstairs.

"She's awake. She's alright." Softly, he stepped into the room. "Hello Ava. You gave us quite a fright."

"What happened?"

"Don't you remember?"

"It all seems rather bleary, like some weird dream."

He was about to answer when Aunt Winifred walked in with Tarran's mother, Meadow. She was a midwife and matron at the local hospital and would gladly tell you she had helped to deliver over a thousand babies.

"Hello darling, we were so worried," Winifred said as she bent down and kissed Ava on the forehead.

"What happened? How did I get back?"

"Jennifer came back alone without you. Her lead had snapped, she would never pull away from you so we knew something was wrong."

"A search party was sent out," chipped in Tarran, perching himself on the corner of Ava's bed. "Mum and I found you."

"You're fine. You were just a little fatigued from everything," Aunt Meadow explained whilst checking Ava's temperature with an ear thermometer. "Plenty of fluids and plenty of rest Ava, and you'll be up and about in no time. Come on Tarran, you can talk later."

Tarran's blue eyes had a softness to their striking beauty. He had inherited his mother's caring compassion. Although he was tall for his age he had a gentleness about him that Ava felt comfortable with, unlike Morgan. He also liked the same things as Ava. He was interested in history and archaeology, had even accompanied Ava and her father last summer on a dig site near the Jurassic coastline in Dorset.

Tarran and Meadow left Ava alone with Winifred who had wandered towards the window. She was picking at her cuticles while staring at the trees and estate.

"What's wrong, auntie?"

Turning to Ava, her concerned expression did nothing for reassurance. "Nothing dear. All's well."

Ava raised one eyebrow.

Winifred flung her hands to her side.

"Well, I'm just so very worried about you and your father. Oh Ava, there is so much I want to tell you, but I can't."

"Why not?"

Sitting back on the bed and gently brushing away Ava's curly hair on her forehead, she replied softly, "Because the time is not right dear. There is a time for everything, and everything has a place."

Ava did not understand. She stared at Aunt Winifred who was indeed a beautiful woman, not marked by the passing of time but matured by its battles. A strength and confidence radiated from her. She was small and petite but when she walked into a room she appeared tall and commanding. Her long white hair had once been golden curls, just like Ava's, and she wore it up most days.

Whenever Ava had accompanied her to town, people had stared after her, such was her presence and beauty. Some would say hello, others would turn away when they saw her coming down the street or run back inside their houses or go back into the shop they'd just stepped from.

Although Ava admired her aunt, she felt uncomfortable with the way people reacted to her, as well as to her other 'aunts'. Fortunately, she had spent little time in the town. When she did come to Candlesby Manor with her father, she stayed on the estate as there was so much to see and do.

The library and armoury were Ava's favourite rooms. She had spent many hours reading, wandering through the house and estate, and playing, especially with Tarran, Morgan and a number of other 'cousins'. Aunt Winifred had no children but out of the thirteen women who lived occasionally at the house, six of them had children, all boys, and all very different.

"You can tell me anything auntie. I'm stronger than I look. Dad always said I can deal with anything."

Winifred bit her bottom lip.

"All in good time. But I will leave you now and rest. Get up when you want to Ava. Chocolate is always available."

"Dear auntie," said Ava with affection.

Aunt Winifred kissed Ava on the forehead and left the room as Jennifer came padding in. She took one look at Ava's bed, jumped up, padded over to her and sniffed, found a comfy spot, turned and flopped down.

Ava was left alone with her thoughts - and Jennifer. She wondered what on earth was going on. She reached for her small leather-bound journal with unlined, blank pages. She needed blank pages to make drawings, sketches and rubbings in, just like her father, the professor.

Ava had to try and make sense of what was going on.

'I need to stick to the facts. Write what I know. Date, time, people, places, when and where. Just write what happened, as it happened, don't make any assumptions. Stick to the facts, just the facts. Res Non Verba,' Ava told herself, quoting her family motto, Facts Not Words. Writing in the journal, she felt in control at last.

The events of the past couple of weeks had left her feeling confused and frightened. Staring at the page in her journal, Ava read what she had written:

Father missing, strange lights, an ancient force.

What was the ancient force?

Next to the words, Ava drew a giant question mark. Who could help her she wondered? She turned the page and wrote the names of the thirteen women - the 'aunts' she had always known:

1   Fawn Grimsbane
2   Alexia Thornton
3   Jissika Ataksak
4   April Brevil
5   Guinevere Shadow
6   Ellie Windrush
7   Ini Straleen
8   Eowyn Labyrinth
9   Briar Moffatt
10   Brenna Monroe
11   Holly Hart
12   Meadow Pickering
13   Winifred Wolfman Fellow

She sat back in bed and stared at the page with no idea as to why these thirteen women would be so close. Why would they always descend upon Candlesby Manor and treat Aunt Winifred as if she were some unnamed leader?

Ava had no idea that these thirteen women, who were not family, had a legacy and responsibility. Yet, none of them were related except by traditions from every continent, from Africa, India, Australia, Europe and New Zealand. These thirteen women were women of the world, united by a mysterious universal code.

Ava was a part of that history. She *was* its past, present and future.

As she stared at the names of the thirteen women, she slouched back surrounded by comfy pillows. Her room was airy and cool, the open window allowed the soft breeze to flow through. She lay dreaming while listening to the bees busying themselves outside and her eyelids felt heavy.

She was only awakened by intermittent gaggles of laughter drifting further and further away from the house. Almost prising her eyes open, Ava could see Jennifer still at the bottom of the bed, sprawled out. As Ava moved, Jennifer's tale immediately started wagging.

"You still here Jennifer?"

Rubbing her eyes, she turned to the clock. Nearly seven. She had slept almost the entire day. Her stomach reminded her that she had only eaten two pieces of toast all day. As she got out of bed, she felt a sudden whoosh and saw the floor rise to meet her.

"I really need to eat something."

She slipped on her denim shorts and stepped into her flipflops, pulled out the T-shirt she had been sleeping in from her shorts and ruffled her hair.

Descending three flights of stairs she could hear someone clattering around in the first kitchen in the basement. She had thought she was alone in the house after hearing all the aunts laughing and giggling as they wondered off into the forest.

Jennifer followed cautiously behind and stopped at the kitchen door. She hid behind Ava's legs. Then her nose rose high into the air and sniffed. Her tail spoke volumes as it wagged furiously. Then she gave a little 'humph!' and bounced on into the kitchen.

Ava slowly peered round the door and gave a sigh of relief.

"Tarran!" she exclaimed.

Tarran swung round from the sink with a colander in his hand.

"Oh hi. You're up? Just thought I'd make dinner."

The delicious aroma wafting through the kitchen made Ava's stomach grumble.

"Smells yummy Tarran, what is it?"

"Bolognaise. You do like pasta, don't you?"

"Yes, of course."

"I thought you did. Hungry?"

"Starving."

"Shall we eat here or in the dining room?"

"Right here's fine, but where are the others?"

Ava glanced around. She didn't want to eat anywhere else, she didn't even want to waste time moving. She wanted food *now*!

"Oh, you know what this place is like at Midsummer," Tarran replied handing Ava forks and spoons.

Clearing the centre island of remnants of tomatoes, herbs

and cheese, Ava nodded.

"Oh yes, when is it?"

"Three weeks time Ava, 21st June remember?"

Tossing the spaghetti into a large bowl and placing on the makeshift table, Tarran added the steaming bolognaise.

"Looks delicious Tarran."

Tarran reached over for the cheese and grater.

"Must have cheese on spaghetti," he said. "Take as much as you want, I've made plenty."

She took a generous helping of spaghetti bolognaise and quickly glanced at Jennifer who was scratting around the kitchen for any remnants of food that might have fallen to the floor. Jennifer was well versed in the art of scratting as she hoovered the perimeter of the kitchen, starting at its cupboards and gradually making her way to the centre where Tarran and Ava sat eating. She stared at them in turn but no luck.

Maybe it was because Ava was famished that the food tasted so utterly delicious. She wanted to savour every moment but she was so hungry that she hardly chewed the food at all.

"This is absolutely scrummy Tarran."

"Thank you," replied Tarran, dipping some fresh bread into the sauce. "I always think the secret to a good bolognaise are the fresh ingredients. And the food grown here at Candlesby House is the best around."

"Where did you learn to cook like this?"

"School. My Home Economics class. I really like it. It's rather refreshing actually, much more enjoyable than Latin or Physics."

"Oh, you like practical lessons? To work with one's hands is a great gift."

Tarran said knowingly, "I am a true labourer. I earn that I eat, get that I wear."

Ava giggled and replied, "Owe no man hate, envy no man's happiness."

All went quiet as Ava peered down at her empty plate.

"Have some more," said Tarran.

"No thanks. I've eaten too much as it is," Ava replied, sitting back in the chair and patting her stomach.

Tarran was just three years older than Ava but was so mature for his age, they both were. The events of the past had made them grow up quicker, although Aunt Meadow did expect a lot from Tarran. His father was an anaesthetist at the local hospital where his mother also worked.

Out of the thirteen women, only Meadow had remained with her husband. The other twelve women were either single mothers or married to each other, single from death, desertion or divorce. And the deaths had been strange. Winifred had said it was the price they pay for being who they were, but as always, she had never elaborated.

"Where have they all gone again Tarran?"

"Into the forest to get the Solstice Heart ready for Midsummer. Would you like to join them?"

Ava hesitated. She didn't want to go into the forest alone again, not after the morning's events. Further, she didn't like the Heart of the Forest, it had a brook running through it, and Ava did not like water, especially 'live' water as she called it.

Tarran noticed her hesitation. "I'll go with you?"

"Oh... ok, thank you. Shall we tidy this up?"

"No leave it, one of the aunts will do it. Let's go."

Tarran opened the door for Ava and then followed her out. They could hear voices in the distance and walked towards them. Jennifer bounced out after them but when it came clear they were headed into the forest once more, she turned back towards the kitchen.

It was early June and the sun was kind. A cloudless evening sky with twilight flowers releasing their heady scents intermittently. It was almost eight and the sun was low in the sky. Ava squinted her eyes at it and wished she had brought her sunglasses. The birds sang loudly and wood pigeons flapped in the tall trees, cooing.

Ava spotted a blue-white feather on the ground. It was too beautiful to have come from a bird, surely? She bent down and picked it up, studied its delicate softness. Its tiny white feathers were so fragile, she wondered how this could ever help a bird to fly. It was paper thin, more like a wing of a butterfly than a bird's feather, perhaps some kind of hybrid between a butterfly and a bird, but what kind of creature had such wings?

Ava placed the feather in her pocket. She would stick it in her journal when she returned to the house.

Approaching the forest, she was apprehensive after the events of the morning but felt safe with Tarran next to her, plus she could hear her aunts not far away. Tarran noticed Ava brushing away something from her face.

"What's the matter?"

"Cobwebs. They're everywhere, in the house, in the garden, in my room. Don't you feel them?"

Tarran stopped in his tracks. He raised his head to look up at the trees. The tops of them had begun to rustle frantically and all the birds had gone quiet. The wind only seemed to be at one place, the tops of the trees, and it was spreading from one tree to another, like dominos falling. Tarran grabbed Ava's hand.

"Run Ava, we must reach the Heart of the Forest. Your aunts will protect you."

"What...?"

It was already too late. Tarran was pulling her through the forest, jumping over bits of fallen trees, snapping twigs and scampering over debris, racing hard.

Turning back briefly, Ava saw with shock a vortex following them, a swirling column of wind, making the leaves dance like a whirling dervish. The trees bent right over to the ground as if made of elastic.

Running and scrambling through the forest debris with the sound of her blood rushing and heart pounding, Ava saw her aunts. They like standing stones in a circle, megalithic monuments of time, gazing out upon a scene of mayhem.

Winifred reached out her hand to Ava who was willing her stretched hand to meet the other, but just as the two connected, Ava's legs were pulled into the air. The wind devil had caught her. She rose higher and higher, as if two hands of ice were holding her ankles, pulling her away, but her aunt and Tarran held her down with strength and determination.

All the women chanted, as one:

"We are the Gatekeepers,

You shall not pass.
Ava will stay fast.

We are the Gatekeepers,
You shall not pass.
Ava will stay fast."

Out of a cloudless sky shot a flash of lightning followed by boom of thunder sending shock waves of vibrating power through the air. The wind devil slowed and stopped.

Ava fell with a thud. Rubbing her ankles, she could see red hand prints on them but no-one had been in the wind devil. It was just a mini tornado. Nothing could possibly be inside it, she reassured herself.

Tarran turned to his mother. Her hand was placed over her heart but it was Lexi who spoke.

"What in Beelzebub's name was that? I think I need some answers, don't you?"

Winifred swallowed and nodded.

4. The Gatekeepers

The women stood in a circle in the Solstice Heart. Winifred spoke:

"We are stronger here Ava. This is the heart of the Forest."

Birds started singing again, masses of them chirping, and a swarm of crows circled and squawked above. Ava ducked, fearing they were swooping down to her. Winifred raised her hands in their defence.

"We are nature Ava and so are they. They mean you no harm darling."

"Then what is that?" Ava demanded, pointing to her ankles. "Just the wind?"

"Nature can play some mean tricks on us."

Winifred wasn't giving anything away so Ava changed tactics.

"What's so special about here then?"

Lexi stepped forward and said, "It's the meeting place for all our services. It has a power of its own." She pointed to the stone table. "Stone – earth," moving her index finger round in a strange shape, Ava watched as Aunt Lexi pointed out things that had always been there. "Aconite or Wolfbane – air, mandrake – fire, the brook – water and Spirit or divinity, the eternity that is the Hemlock Tree. They all form to make a penta..."

"That's enough Lexi." Winifred raised her hand. "You've said enough."

Lexi lowered her head.

"Let's go back to the house and discuss this over dinner. You must be hungry Ava?"

"I've already eaten," Ava replied sharply, but immediately regretted her behaviour. "Thank you," she added.

The other Aunts had begun to scurry back to the house. Tarran turned to Ava. "Shall we go back?"

"Thank you Tarran. I'm tired. I think I will go to bed early." Ava strolled past Winifred and Lexi, staring at them both.

Tarran gestured for Ava to go first and Ava nodded courtly to him, like a princess.

Walking back to the house, Ava's brow was furrowed, so many questions were racing through her mind. Tarran glanced at her, pursing his lips. He felt compelled to defend his mother and the aunts.

"Don't be too hard on Aunt Winifred, Ava. She's doing her best. She's only behaving like this to keep you safe."

"Safe! Safe from what?"

Tarran didn't answer.

"What danger am I in? What was that? Why doesn't anyone tell me?"

"There are more things in heaven and Earth Horatio, than are dreamt of in your philos…"

"Oh, enough with the Shakespeare, Tarran. I want some answers and don't tell me you don't know what's going on."

"There's magic at work Ava, plain and simple."

She did not believe it.

"How can you of all people say that?" Tarran asked.

"Well, I can and I have," Ava replied, but then realised what Tarran had said. "What do you mean, me of all people?"

"We're nearly home," Tarran replied, trying to change the subject, but Ava was having none of these diversionary tactics.

"Go on, what do you mean, me of all people?"

Tarran hesitated, then said, "Well, your family being so ancient and …"

"And?"

"You're all practitioners…"

"Yes?"

"Of magic," Tarran sighed. "You are all practitioners of The Craft. You are all witches, Ava."

"Don't be ridiculous, my father isn't a witch. He's an archaeologist as well you know. And as for my mother… I don't know about her, but Aunt Winifred, well… maybe… she's different, yes, I grant you that, and a bit strange, but a *witch*?"

Ava tried to work out what it all meant as she babbled on. "And what about your mother? What does it make her?"

"She's a witch, too. Many of the witches of the past were

midwives. My mother is just following family tradition. But all the aunts are part of The Thirteen."

"Thirteen?"

"The Thirteen sacred families who are the Gatekeepers, protectors of the Earthly Realms."

Ava stopped still outside the house and stared straight up at Tarran.

"I thought you were different, but you're all completely crackers."

"Ava…" Tarran started to say.

"No! Leave me alone. I'm tired and want to go to bed."

She did not wait for Tarran's reply. She marched on into the house, ignoring the aunts who had already arrived home. She stomped upstairs to her room.

Jennifer was snoozing at the bottom of Ava's bed. She opened one eye and immediately her tail started wagging. Ava greeted her and patted her head.

"Go back to sleep sweetie. You can't help me, nobody can."

Jennifer closed her eye, and her tail went still.

Ava put her hands in her pocket remembering the feather. Pulling it out of her denim shorts, she held it in the palm of her hand. Carefully, she traced its fragile lines and marks with her index finger. As she went over it, the feather gave a sort of spark. She stared at the palm of her hand. The feather seemed to radiate a blue glow and trembled. She cupped her hands around it to watch, fearing it would fly off.

As quickly as the spark had come, the light faded. The energy had left, its battery had died. 'Wish I had my microscope with me.'

She picked up her journal and opened it at the last written page. The thirteen women's names stared back at her.

Ava flopped down onto the bed, still holding the feather and journal. She picked up the pen and next to the thirteen she wrote what she knew about them. 'Just the facts Ava. Just the facts,' she reminded herself, where the women were from, the children they'd had and whether they'd incurred the 3D's of death, desertion or divorce.

When she'd finished, she sat back and studied the page. She

placed the feather inside the journal and closed it. Resting her head on the pillow, she closed her eyes and drifted into a light slumber.

Night was beginning to fall when she sat bolt upright, jolted by a sudden thought. Aunts Winifred and Lexi had not yet returned from the Heart of the Forest. Ava would have heard them, surely. She rushed to the window. The sky was still light, not quite pitch black. 'I wonder...,' she thought.

She turned to Jennifer.

"What do you think Jen? Do you think I can get back to the Solstice Heart before night fall?"

Jennifer raised her head to glance at Ava but it was far too heavy and fell back onto the soft quilt. Ava would have to creep past the other aunts and Tarran but they were busying themselves about the house. It could be done.

"Right! Let's do it."

Slipping off her flipflops, Ava ran barefoot to the door and tiptoed down the stairs, stopping every now and then to look-out for aunts. Hiding behind the bannister, she could see the door. The coast was clear and she made a run for it.

She dashed across the daisy lawn to the forest. Only when she was in the clear did she put her flipflops back on before scurrying through the forest to its heart.

'Rubbish!' she told herself. 'There is nothing out here. It was the wind, a mini tornado I got caught up in."

She was so lost in thoughts, Lexi almost saw her, but she dived into bushes behind the solstice heart and listened.

"Are you going to tell her?"

"Tell her?"

"Everything."

"Everything? Don't be ridiculous, Lexi. How can I? She's a child after all."

"She's not just a child, she's *his* child, and she's a lot stronger than you think."

"This should not have happened. This should not be happening to her."

"Well, it is, so deal with it. You should tell her... well, maybe not all, but she needs to know the truth and she needs to know what exactly she's dealing with. Forewarned is forearmed."

"Lexi, once and for all, this should not be happening. She is a child and this is not her responsibility to find him and bring him back to our world. We closed all the doorways many years ago to keep her safe."

"They obviously found a way to open them."

"No, there's something else going on, something more sinister. I felt it many moons ago. Have you heard him at night, screeching? He's looking for something."

"Ava?"

"I don't know… we have to protect her, we have a responsibility. We are both gatekeepers to the other worlds. We have a duty to protect all."

"Yes, but we are also mediators between Earth and all therein. Can we not mediate and intervene before it's too late?"

"We can try but I fear it is already too late. Things have been set in motion now and there is only one path before us. The path that Ava must go down."

"Alone?"

"Alone! But I still say this should not be happening. What happened, Lexi? Did we do something to anger them?"

"Whatever we have done or not done, she needs to be told everything."

"Everything? Everything is still too much for a child, and not only that, remember, whatever we are dealing with now was powerful enough to punch a hole in this world and take Riley with it. I don't know what hovers over us, but there is much danger here. I've never felt a force like it. We all need to work together on this before it destroys everything we hold dear and everyone we love. There is much evil Lexi, and it grows stronger every day."

"May the gods help us."

"May they indeed, so mote it be."

"So mote it be!"

Ava leant forward further to hear but missed her footing and stumbled snapping twigs and rustling leaves.

She whispered a soft curse as she fell back through the trees.

Lexi and Winifred stopped as if turned to stone. "Perhaps we should leave?"

"Yes. Let's return to the house."

Ava was frightened to breathe as she crouched down in the forest brush, protected by elderberry blossom and hawthorn bushes. She watched with curiosity as her two aunts paced back to the house until she felt it was safe to come out of hiding. She stood and surveyed the Solstice Heart, the Heart of the Forest. What had Aunt Lexi been trying to say when Winifred shut her down?

She wandered over to the stand, thirteen stone chairs surrounding a round stone table, the wolfbane, the mandrake, the brook, the Hemlock Tree all in a strange shape. Ava tried to work it out, drawing imaginary lines to each of these five points. What shape has five points?

A pentagram!

Relieved she had discovered something, she raised her head to the sky as if to thank it. There was not a breeze and the clouds were grey and heavy. So heavy, Ava thought that the sky would fall upon her. The air was hot and humid yet Ava felt a chill within her. Why had she not brought a coat? She scolded her unpreparedness.

Something rustled on the forest floor, too loud and firm to be a bird. It sounded like small stomps through the fallen leaves and broken twigs of summer storms. She walked back to the house but it seemed to be following her.

She walked faster and so did the echoing steps. It scurried through the forest brush trying to keep up with Ava whose run had become a sprint.

"Oh, vanilla sprinkles, I can't do this. I give up."

Ava stopped dead in her tracks. She had not imagined that voice, like someone speaking with helium in their lungs. She strained her eyes to see and something jumped into the air. A tree branch pinged but it wasn't the wind that had blown it. Something had held it back and let go.

'I have nothing to fear, remember what Aunt Winifred said, everything will be alright,' Ava told herself before closing her eyes and shouting, "Who's there?"

Nothing.

"I said, who's there? Show yourself. I command you?"

Ava opened her eyes to see a small blue dancing flame growing as it pulsated, creating a slow hum. It was not an electronic hum, more the sound a bee would make.

As it grew, feet appeared, then a body, then an exquisite little face and finally the source of the sound itself, a beautiful pair of beating wings. Cascading colours of blues, greens, edges of white, like the feather Ava had found.

"Hello," it said, and sort of a gave a half bow to Ava who had neither blinked nor breathed.

The little creature sorted of tutted, shrugged its shoulders and repeated louder, "Hello?"

Ava remembered to breathe.

"Hello," she exhaled. "Who are you?"

"George."

"George?"

"Yes, George," the little creature replied.

"George?"

"Is there an echo in here? Yes, that's my name."

"But you're a... fairy!"

"Let me guess. You were expecting Buttercup, Thistle, Daisy?"

Ava did not know how to respond. She could feel the events of the past weeks swell up inside her until finally she exclaimed, "This is too much! I'm having a nervous breakdown, it's finally happened."

"Oh, lemon sherbets, you are so dramatic!"

Ava stared at George aghast, not believing what she was seeing.

"I've been through so much, my father's disappearance, the strange whirlwind, the lights, the noises at night..."

George tried to intervene.

"Yes, yes, about those, inexplicable things will happen around you – can't be avoided. You need to come with me Ava and all will be revealed. Or some of it, at least."

"No, I won't. It's not true."

"Not what you were expecting then?" George's face broke

into a crooked smile. "Expecting a white rabbit wearing a tweed waistcoat and carrying a pocket watch, were we?"

"Well…"

George clicked his wings and zap, he turned into a white rabbit. He started scurrying around exclaiming, "I'm late, I'm late," in a mock Mr Rabbit - Alice in Wonderland voice before clicking his wings again and returning to the magnificent being he was.

"Lewis Carroll felt the same way," said George, seeing Ava's astonishment. "Look we really haven't got time for any of this. It's getting late and Midsummer will soon be upon us. We need to go."

"Go where?"

"Avalonia. We have an audience with royalty," and George scouted round their surroundings.

"Avalonia? Av… what are you looking for?"

"Found it, star jasmine," and George flew over to a white flowered plant. Picking several, he bowed to the plant and said, "Thank you, Lady." He then proceeded to fly over Ava's head and shook the plants all over her. Golden dust fell all around her. He then held the bunch up and said, "Smell," but before she had time or space to refuse, Ava had taken one giant sniff and sneezed.

Everything went black, her ears popped and she felt like she was falling, falling, endlessly.

"Hold on to my hand Ava, here we go."

"Here we go where?" she cried in desperation. "Where are you taking me?"

"As I said," replied George, "Avalonia."

5. Avalonia

Ava could feel George's tiny hand, so delicate and fragile like his wings. Humans don't know their own strength or the damage they can do to a being of nature.

Ava was spinning and spinning yet falling at the same time. Her eyes were tightly closed and when she did open one for a brief moment she was surrounded by blackness. There was nothing to see with her eyes but she could see with her body - the feelings, the smells, the sounds and the tastes.

As George wrapped his little hand round her finger, a feeling of pins and needles shot through her body. As she spun round she could feel shockwaves of electricity running through her, like thousands of tiny fairy feet skipping up and down her spine.

She spun, fell and heard a whooshing, shushing sound permeating through her, around her and all over her like torrents of water. Yet she was not wet as she padded herself to make sure she was warm and dry.

The smells were odd. At one point, as she was spinning and falling, twisting and turning, she would enter pockets of different smells – a fragrance of flowers, to trees, to cut grass and summer rain, to the smell of chocolate chip cookies baking or the sweetness of a fairground, of toffee apples and candyfloss.

The taste upon her lips was not that of such sweet delicacies, but salt - salt of the seaside. She half expected to hear sea gulls squawking but she did not. Instead, all the feelings, sounds, tastes and aromas created an image in her mind's eye of going through a vortex or energy portal, like those she had read about in her father's science magazines, an energy portal connecting to another dimension - one that would take her to Avalonia!

A land, a world, she had never heard of.

The sounds and feelings changed from whooshing and shushing to the soft ring of tiny bells and delicate harmonies on the breath of distant winds.

The air felt like soft petals of buttercups caressing your skin on a warm summer's day. The smell was the smell of elder blossom and honeysuckle. The taste was no longer salt but the sweetest honey on the lips.

Ava had arrived.

6. Believe

Ava felt George release his grip on her finger.

"Open your eyes slowly Ava. The lights are very difficult to see for the first time."

"The lights?"

"Human eyes find them hard to comprehend."

Ava opened her eyes gradually. The tiniest amount of light flood into them forcing her to close them immediately. She rubbed them, it was so painful.

"You have to grow accustomed to them."

"But it's dazzling, George."

"It is the light of innocence. It is the light of the beginning, the light of lights. Human eyes cannot look upon this for too long or they will go blind."

Ava tried once more to open her eyes, slowly, all the while squinting. The light of Avalonia was a glaze of white over everything. This world stemmed from the deepest source of knowledge and traditions. Its light was a fluid veil over the environment.

Ava rubbed her eyes. She wished she had her sunglasses with her. Once more she was unprepared.

Avalonia appeared as a dream, a mist over sight, a haze that could not be cleared. It hung heavy in the air like an early summer morning when the horizon glowed in a veil of white dew.

Ava could feel her skin glistening as if she was walking through a gentle shower, though her clothes were not wet. Even the breeze could not alter the sunrise yellow haze of day.

She stopped and listened, for within that soft breeze she could hear voices carried. Glancing towards the trees, she saw their leaves and branches sway but she could not hear their rustling. All that could be heard were voices upon the air, whispers, words dancing upon the breeze like crickets jumping to an everlasting song of summer.

"Welcome Ava."

"Ava's here!"

"She's come home!"

"Do you think the lady knows she's home?"

"Do you hear that?"

George raised his head and buzzed his wings.

"Hear what?"

"Voices… welcoming me home."

"Marvellous! Excellent! Very very nice! Now we really must make haste to the Great Hall. No time for sightseeing on this trip, Ava. The King and Queen are most anxious to meet with you." George studied Ava up and down. "You're not intending to wear that are you?"

Offended, Ava replied, "What do you mean? I wasn't intending on meeting royalty today, and besides, I don't have any dresses. I wear jeans, shorts and T-shirts."

"Tut, tut! Don't you even have a school uniform?"

"I don't go to school. I'm home schooled. My father or the other archaeologists and scientists we work with teach me."

"Tut again! Well, you can't go looking like that, now can you?"

Ava folded her arms. She liked her shorts and slept in her T-shirt.

"What's your favourite colour?"

"Yellow."

"Good choice, mine too. Let's see now," and George flew around her, measuring with his fairy hands like he was playing charades taking a picture. "Now this should be about right. Snip, snap, pop, snap, snip, shop."

George clicked his wings and in a flash Ava was transformed from a shorts-and-T-shirt-flip-flop-girl into an elegant princess ready to meet a King and Queen.

The dress was yellow and cream with layers of lace and silk cut into an asymmetrical skirt. One side was knee length whilst the other fell almost to her ankle. Her flip-flops had changed into daffodil yellow satin ankle boots with dainty Louis heels.

"Perfect! As befitting royalty."

"Wow! Oh, thank you George," swirled Ava, who felt

especially swishy.

George beamed with pride.

"Full on Avalonia New Wave with a touch of Mermaid Mash-up."

Ava stared at him, confused.

"Our fashion styles here in Avalonia."

"Oh," nodded Ava whilst reaching for her hair which had been braided in the front, entwined with daisies and buttercups. The flowered braid went around her blond hair like a crown. At the back, her hair cascaded down like a waterfall with intermittent daisies and buttercups throughout.

'I wonder what Tarran would say if he saw me?' she thought to herself, and forgot that he had made her angry. She wished Tarran was with her now, here in Avalonia.

"We must be going, Ava. Their majesties are waiting for us in the Great Hall."

"Is it a long way?"

"Not for fairies," and George rustled his wings. "But for humans, it's a hop, skip and a jump on the Cloud of Believing."

George clicked his wings and a wondrous blue cloud appeared before Avam fluffy, swirling and mysterious.

"Now then, hop on."

"What?"

"Hop, skip, jump remember."

Ava wobbled as she positioned herself to hop onto cloud.

"Are you sure?"

"This is Avalonia. I am sure."

"When I wake up, I'm going straight to the doctor."

George tutted and rolled his eyes. "So dramatic."

Ava closed her eyes as she took one large hop onto the cloud which instantly rolled away. Ava fell to the floor with a crash.

"Ouch! What the…"

"Stop that!" George scolded the cloud. "You know who Ava is, stop it and behave yourself." Turning to Ava George apologetically said, "I'm sorry, he has a tendency to be a bit of a joker. Please try again."

Ava pressed her lips together, positioned herself again,

standing on one leg. This time she kept her eyes open as she took one huge hop onto the cloud which was still wriggling slightly and making a whimpering noise. Standing on it was extraordinary. By rights, Ava should have sunk through the formless gas, but she didn't. The cloud cradled her in tendrils of white mist.

"Now you need to skip."

"What?"

"Skip. You do know how to skip don't you?"

"Of course, I know how to skip but if I do, I'll fall off."

"Just skip, three should do it."

"Do what?"

"Do it now, skip!"

"Alright, alright keep your wings on. I'll skip just to prove you wrong."

Ava prepared to fall off the cloud as she skipped, one, two, three. The cloud flew at an unbelievable speed until it came to a sudden stop, jerking her forward.

The scenery had completely changed. She was surrounded by hundreds of fairies - large, small, red, yellow, green and blue, a multitude of rainbow colours danced before her eyes. Their wings had a life of their own as they swirled around. The hustle and bustle of a fairy city overshadowed by a huge great gold building that shimmered in the unique light of Avalonia.

"We're here."

"Truly? That was quick," said Ava, reeling slightly from the wondrous transportation.

"Fairy speed. You've heard of the speed of light well, this is the speed of fae. Different, but just as nifty. Now you need to jump off."

Ava stepped off the cloud. Immediately, it sped away to its next destination leaving nothing behind but a memory. One blink and the Cloud of Believing was gone.

7. The Hieroglyphic Fae

Ava opened her lips to speak but was stopped abruptly by George who said, as he rushed passed her, "We are going to be late. Their majesties do not like to be kept waiting. Hurry!" and the little being flapped his wings and clapped his tiny hands. "Come along, come *along*!"

Ava wanted to stop and look at everything but the magnificent palace doors of golden sunlight rays and white marble inlays beckoned. They creaked open giving a sight few mortals had seen - a huge corridor of cascading colours, a line with images of monarchs and fae. Ava stumbled along gazing at every picture until she came to a portrait she recognised - Elizabeth I.

"Yes, yes," said George seeing her hesitate, "she was one of the few human monarchs of England to have known about us and our world. Now we really must move along Ava."

He flapped his little wings once more, waved to her and gulped.

"The Throne Room!"

George closed his eyes as he made a strange sign on the door. The huge doors of purest white and green marble heaved open. It was Connemara marble. Ava would recognise it anywhere. Candlesby Manor's kitchen tops were made of it. She had been told by Aunt Brenna that it held special healing powers. Ava had not believed her but she wished Aunt Winifred was with her now as she ventured into the throne room.

Nothing could have prepared Ava for the sight that lay before her. A massive golden room resplendent with mirrors and windows that allowed the light of Avalonia to filter through, twist and cascade down. Ava was reminded of the light in her bedroom.

Beautiful Fae adorned each aisle as they flew to one side creating a path for Ava towards the King and Queen. All was quiet except for the gentle buzz of tiny fairy wings.

George bowed his head to Ava and ushered her forward. She felt like a Princess and was relieved she was no longer wearing her shorts and T-shirt.

She swallowed as she ventured down the long path towards the King and Queen who sat on two huge thrones adorned with shining jewels, but Ava couldn't see the royal features from there, only two glowing orbs of golden light surrounded by flashes of colour from the precious stones adorning their thrones.

As she walked closer to their majesties, she passed fairies on either side who bowed their heads gracefully, whispering in tiny voices. It was the strange language her father had always said existed. A language only spoken by the Enchanted Realm, the other world, another dimension.

Lining her path were not just fairies but all manner of elemental beings. One in particular seemed to stare the longest at Ava. She was taller than the others with fair skin and bright white hair. The clothes she wore were a similar fashion to Ava's. The skirt was definitely a mermaid mash-up and the top seemed to shimmer like it had a life of its own. Yet while Ava was in yellow, hers was the deepest ocean blues. As she passed the strange but stunningly beautiful being, Ava felt uneasy.

She focused her gaze in front of her as their majesties now came into view. She could see now that the thrones were not encrusted with priceless jewels but flowers - forget-me-nots shone like sapphires, red poppies sparkled like rubies and the green ivy which twisted round the thrones gleamed like emeralds.

Approaching the royal pair, Ava could see their glow disappear as she became a part of their light whilst their majesties appeared in their own luminescence. A glistening force field shimmered into the room, and the closer Ava approached, the more she became part of it.

She stopped and curtseyed, impressed with herself. She never thought she could curtsey and turned to George to give a know-all expression, but as she did so, she was dazzled by a fierce royal light.

"Do not be alarmed Ava. We have been waiting for you so

long child."

George flew forward.

"Ah yes, about that, your Majesty…"

"Thank you, George, there's no need for an explanation on the matter," said the King.

George instantly went quiet and bowed his head as he flew back behind Ava.

The King was everything you would expect a King to be except he had wings and was no bigger than a hedgehog. The Queen had pretty, dainty features, so regal.

"We are honoured to have you with us, Ava. Our only sadness is the circumstances which brought you here."

"Well, spoken wife. Yes, ghastly business. Your father has always been an ally of ours," and the King shook his head as his wings lowered.

Ava stepped closer to them.

"What do you mean, 'ghastly business'? Do you know something of my father your Majesty?"

Before he could answer, the Queen flew down from her throne to Ava.

"He is a prisoner here child, captured by such an evil powerful force that even we, the Fae, cannot set him free."

"We are prisoners here as much as he is," added the King.

"What do you mean?" Ava asked

"There is an evil presence in the world. A heavy, foreboding has descended such that children, adults and animals no longer believe."

"I'm sorry, animals?"

"We are all connected Ava. We all beat with the same lifeforce. What affects one, affects us all. Will you help us Ava? Will you help bring back our knowledge to the world? Will you help us destroy this terrible presence?"

The Queen fluttered around Ava, her golden wings beating so fast that an enchanting lullaby could be heard permeating the room until all the elemental beings joined in a beautiful harmony.

The King flew down and joined his wife. His wings gave the song a deeper sound. Swaying round Ava, he said, "Will you help us restore the realm and free your father? Will you?"

8. A Sacred Language

Ava stood in this mighty hall and could hear expectation in the silence. Only one word came to mind. "How?"

"That's easy Ava," said the King. "You need to learn the language, but you - a daughter of ours - this language is a part of you. Your father wrote it in his journal, which I'm afraid sealed his fate."

"Why?"

"Knowledge Ava, sacred ancient knowledge. We keep secret. Your world is too dark for the light of understanding to return."

Ava bore a little diamond crease of worry on her forehead when she was confused. George could see she was struggling.

"Perhaps your majesties, if I could intercede?"

The King appeared unamused.

"Ava needs to learn our language but to do so slowly, naturally. You want her to learn by doing?"

"Yes. Quite. Quite."

"We have not time to send Ava to Saille-Posh for wa-wa-wa yanni."

Ava did a double take.

"Saille-Posh wa...? What's all that?"

"That is the language of the Fae, or as you would call us, fairies. Your father wrote about it - The Sacred Language of Fairies," said George.

"I suggest you read it young lady," commanded the King.

George was growing impatient.

"May I also add that Yap will soon be upon us. We really have little time your Majesty."

"Yes, quite true Commander Wrenn."

The Queen flew close to Ava who could feel the wisps of air caressing her face from the beat of her majesty's delicate wings.

"Ava," the Queen asked, "will you help us? Will you rescue

your father and in so doing free our realm from the terrible presence that hovers over both our worlds?"

Ava didn't need to think; her answer was swift.

"Yes, your Majesty. I would be honoured to complete such a noble task," and she bowed her head, upon which an almighty cheer arose from the Throne Room as all the astonishing beings clapped their tiny hands and cheered and whistled. The Queen returned the bow to Ava before flying back to her throne.

"Now know this," the room fell silent as the King spoke. "To all those who can hear my voice and all those around our realm, Ava is to be given every help and support from Fae to Dragon to Mermaid to Unicorn alike. She will journey far in her quest. She is our bravest warrior. She is fighting to free us from this darkness. We all know whose daughter she is and therefore, she commands the highest respect as she too is royalty."

Ava realised how famous her father was her.

"Commander Wrenn."

"Yes Sir."

"You are to accompany Ava on this quest. You are to teach and guide her in our ways. Help her as much as possible. But know this George, she is royalty, her commands must be obeyed."

"Yes Sir," and George clicked his wings to attention.

"And whatever you do Commander Wrenn, keep her safe."

"Sir," George nodded and bowed.

Seeing the great challenge of her quest, Ava said, "Please your Majesties... where do I begin? How do I find my father?"

"Commander Wrenn will help you. Follow your instincts and always trust your first thought. Know that time and skill go with you. The prophecy has been fulfilled."

"The prophecy?"

When Thirteen Treasures become one.
Then meet on battlefield Fae and human.
The Celtic Messiah will arise.
To chase the darkness from our eyes.

"The Celtic Messiah?" Ava asked.

"The Son of Prophecy," said the Queen, "the one who will fight for our realms and worlds. Go now and begin the quest that will fulfil your destiny. Trust no-one. The darkness is a master of deceit and those you trust as allies could be your enemy. Go with time and ability. Midsummer will soon be upon us. Blessings upon you."

The Queen bowed once more to Ava when, without warning, her fairy form faded. A thick haze rose from the floor and swept through the Throne Room. The King silently acknowledged her then he too faded and vanished.

The entire ensemble of fantastic beings dissolved and disappeared.

"We shall see each other again Ava," said the being who had greeted her minutes earlier, then she too melted away into nothingness.

Before Ava could ask George what was happening, she found herself back in the stone circle, in the Heart of the Forest, but it was no longer night. The sun was beginning to rise over the horizon and the blackbird was singing its morning song.

9. The Awakening

"What was all that about George, or should I say Commander Wrenn?"

George was sheepish.

"You wouldn't have believed me if I had told you. You do not believe. You do not believe in anything at all unless you can see it, hear it or feel it."

"That's not true. All manner of things exist that I don't see but I know they are there."

"Like what?"

"Gravity, electricity, magnetic energy..."

"Energy?"

"Yes."

"Do you believe we are all connected in this way?"

"I don't know, George. All I do know is that I have to rescue my father, battle the darkness that's covering our worlds and find thirteen treasures, all by Midsummer."

"And even there you are wrong."

"What? That's what the King and Queen said. And by the way, I don't even know their names!"

"That's where your education shall begin. You don't have to do everything before Midsummer but do need to have at least one of the treasures by then."

"We haven't a moment to lose, have we?" Ava swiftly started to stomp back towards the house.

Ava realised she no longer felt uneasy in the Heart of the Forest. Somehow, the stone circle no longer frightened her, but she suddenly stopped dead in her tracks and George almost flew into her. Ava's face had turned white with fear. George followed her stare upwards towards the sky, just above Candlesby House.

"What... oh, I see. Alexia Thornton is getting a bit of flying practice in," he said. "Everything Tarran told you is correct. Open your eyes Ava, awake to the world around you and see for the first time."

Ava imagined the scene once more. She could see Aunt Lexi circling the house on a broom, gracefully descending towards them.

"You'd better make yourself scarce George."

"Why?"

"Well, you know, you being… a…"

"Ava, you've just been to the enchanted realm of the Fae and now you've seen your aunt flying on a broomstick. Your family are all witches. You must believe that. And you?"

"What am I?"

"Royalty," said George.

"You must do better than that," Ava tutted, rolled her eyes and continued walking.

All the aunts had come out to meet her, Aunt Winifred leading the pack.

"My dear girl, we have been so worried."

"Auntie this is…"

"George! My old friend, lovely to see you again."

George flew past Ava, nudging her.

"Winifred Wolf-moon Fellow. My goodness, its been too long, your grace."

"Dear George, Commander Wrenn, welcome back," Aunt Lexi added as the other aunts joined in the chorus of praise to the fairy hovering before them.

Ava could feel anger welling up inside her. Ignored again.

"Don't mind me," she barged past the old friends and headed inside.

Tarran was waiting for her at the staircase. Ava lowered her head, remembering how she had last spoken to him.

"I'm sorry for earlier on," she whispered, "I spoke out of turn and in haste."

"No need for apologies between friends. We are all entitled to our opinions and friends respect each other's."

He might have been three years older but did he have to be so mature for his age!

The aunts returned with George in tow. Ava watched them, wondering.

"You look lovely Ava," Aunt Meadow said, trying to ease the atmosphere.

"You owe me an explanation," said Ava.

"Right," agreed Aunt Winifred. "In the library, everyone. We have to discuss this. Now."

They made their way into the library with Tarran, George and Aunt Winifred leading the way. In the library, they all had their places sitting on huge leather sofas. Books adorned every wall. Tarran sat next to his mother whilst Aunt Winifred stood in the centre with George beside her. Ava stood opposite. Aunt Winifred took a deep breath.

"We're all witches, my dear Ava. We come from a unique line. Our families have a kind of sorcery running through our veins, not just of England, Ireland, Scotland and Wales but of Africa with Aunt Ellie Windrush, Jamaica with Aunt Ini Straleen and the Inuit of Canada with Aunt Jissika Ataksak.

"Our families have been united for many centuries. We are the thirteen protectors, Gatekeepers of this world and others. We make sure that balance remains in each of the realms. Our ancestry represents all the corners of the earth. We are priestesses for each point of the compass."

"Thirteen?" Ava asked.

"Perhaps this could wait for another day, your grace," George whispered to Aunt Winifred who politely ignored him.

"Thirteen? Like The Thirteen Treasures?" Ava interrupted.

Aunt Winifred swiftly turned to George.

"The Thirteen Treasures? She knows? Has she been commanded to find them?"

Ava interrupted again.

"Yes, and to find my father, not to mention saving the world."

"Ava has been given that responsibility?"

George nodded to Aunt Winifred who stood silent and shocked.

"So it begins," added Aunt Brenna.

"Let the quest start," concurred Aunt Lexi.

10 The Quest

Composing herself, Aunt Winifred plopped herself down on one of the huge leather chairs. She pinched the bridge of her nose.

"Just what exactly was said, Ava? Start from the beginning."

"There is a terrible evil facing our worlds, not just our world but the world of Fae. The Thirteen Treasures must be returned so the Son of Prophecy can return. What I don't understand is how? Why? And what on earth am I going to do?"

Ava slumped to the floor, shoulders hunched. Aunt Winifred bent down and took her face in her hands.

"My darling girl never be afraid, for you have so much potential within you. Learn to channel your fears, be brave and you shall prevail."

"How, auntie, how?"

"The Thirteen Treasure..." Aunt Winifred stopped and turned to Aunt Lexi. "Bring us the book."

"Is it actually happening, Winifred?"

"Could it be?" Aunt Meadow repeated..

The tension in the room was broken with the scurrying steps of Aunt Lexi who handed a book to Winifred.

"What's that?" Ava asked.

"Our history and your future, my darling. It is called the Book of Shadows or a Grimoire," Aunt Winifred answered, searching through the old faded pages of this heavy book. "Yes, here it is."

The aunts leaned in closer to hear. Tarran sat next to Ava on the floor. Reaching out his hand, she felt the warmth of his fingers fold round hers.

"Here," Aunt Winifred read, "the exact location of The Thirteen Treasures is unknown but legend has it that the Keepers met in the North and were persuaded to hand over the Treasures so they could forever be stored in the Castle of Glass.

Legend holds that if The Thirteen Treasures were ever brought back to this mortal world then Son of Prophecy, the Celtic Messiah, would arise."

"The Castle of Glass, the North, but where exactly?"

"What are The Thirteen Treasures, auntie?"

Aunt Winifred continued.

"The Thirteen Treasures are the Horn of Bran, the Sword of Rhyddech the Generous, the Hamper of Gwyddho Long Shanks, the Chariot of Morgan the Wealthy, the Halter of Clyddho Eiddyn."

"Isn't there a cauldron somewhere, Winnie?"

"Yes, the Cauldron of Dyrnwich the Giant, the Knife of Llawfrodedel the Horseman, the Whetstone of Tudwal, the Cloak of Padarn Baisnot." She gestured towards Aunt Meadow. "The Crock of Rhgerydd, the Dish of Rhgenydd, the Chess Board of Gwenddolau and the Mantle of Arthur."

Aunt Winifred let out a puff of air and relaxed.

"The Mantle of Arthur?"

"The Arthur, as in King Arthur?" Tarran added.

"Yes, him."

"So, this is like our own Holy Grail? But that's fiction, it doesn't exist." George cleared his throat and flapped his wings. "Okay, George, I see you, so if you exist, I suppose the Grail could, too. But where do I start?"

Leaning forward to pick up the book once more, Winifred replied, "There's a footnote, C.F. Desiderata."

In unison, Ava and Tarran answered, "Conferred Desiderata."

Winifred was impressed and frantically searched the pages. She stopped at a colourful plate which listed, 'Things That are Yearned For'. She scrolled down them.

"Wisdom, Balance, Health, Truth. Truth, let's see," and she turned the ancient pages again, intently, until stopping at a page headed:

Truth: The Thirteen Treasures.

She cleared her throat:

In echoed steeped darkness
Shines the light from a Dean's Eye,
Left from a Saint's shrine
Where pilgrims meet for communion wine.
Follow the imp backwards in time
Where a Bishop sleeps, a direct line,
The symbol of a Tudor ship you shall find.

Silence.

"Dean's Eye?" repeated Tarran.

"Bishop sleeps?" added Meadow.

More silence, then, "We need chocolate!" clapped Lexi and off she went to raid the breakfast room.

Brenna stood looking over Winifred's shoulder at the page.

"We need to write this down, Winnie. Where's the flipchart?"

Brenna and Fawn hurried out to fetch it.

"What else do you need Winnie?" Aunt Holly asked. She had been sat this entire time, quiet, unassuming, ever present and ever watchful. Ava often thought Aunt Holly like an owl, aware of everything but not making a move, just swooping in when needed.

"Time."

"That's what the King said. He said time and skill go with me."

"He did, did he?" Winifred asked.

"What did he mean?" asked Holly.

Winifred stared into the book.

"He meant that he has given you the gift of time and the power of the Fae. You will be able to transcend time and make every moment yours, even to last a lifetime. But you must learn how to use these gifts as they can have a way of manifesting their own will on the owner."

Ava lowered her head.

"There's so much I don't understand."

George flew close.

"You will learn Ava. You are not alone in this quest. We are

46

all with you."

Clatterings and bangings echoed around the otherwise silent library as Brenna and Fawn stumbled into the door carrying the flip chart .

"Oops! Sorry Winn."

"No worries ladies. Here, pop it in the centre so we can all see."

Lexi followed them with the breakfast basket laden full of chocolate. She handed out bars to everyone as Brenna copied the rhyme down so all could see. Meadow searched the shelves for books on history, Thirteen Treasures and the Celts. Holly made a space for Ava and Tarran on the sofa and patted the cushion. She wrapped her arm round Ava and said, "Never fear, we are all here for you."

Yet Ava had never felt so alone and for the first time in her life she wished she had known her mother. The women worked in harmony, knowing what the others needed, like a military action, swift, silent and graceful.

The aunts dissected the clue line by line, gently pulling apart its words to view the meaning inside.

"Right. Saint's shrine. Where are Saint's buried?"

"Could be anywhere."

"Churches, cathedrals."

"Communion wine… definitely a church or cathedral."

"Dean's Eye?"

"Lincoln Cathedral," said Tarran. "It has the famous Dean's Eye, a stained-glass window, priceless in its beauty and reverence."

"Yes, of course, Lincolnshire! The imp, the symbol of the county," added Aunt Meadow.

"The first clue is in Lincoln, so that is where you must start, Ava."

"But what am I searching for? Which treasure do I go after first? And where? I can't search an entire city."

"I don't know my darling but follow the clues."

"Auntie…"

"Do not fret Ava, George will be with you."

"So will I," Tarran squeezed her hand. "I will journey north with them, Winifred. I'll book the tickets now. We will go by train so we can research as we travel."

Lexi switched the computer on. They might be witches, but the twenty first century had a wonder of its own.

"We will need a full coven, Winnie."

"Yes, they will be here by Litha, maybe sooner. We must be on our guard. We are stronger together. I will go to Wales and gather the others."

"We shall return to Ireland, notify everyone and bring them up to speed. We'll stop off in Scotland and the Hebrides first and let the others know, including Jissika."

"Good," said Winifred. "Excellent."

"But why don't you just phone them, auntie?"

"Because this information is dangerous, Ava. Who knows whether we are being listened to over the phone, or our messages read. These are dangerous times. Our enemies are everywhere."

11. Enemies Everywhere

Standing at the platform, Winifred tried to hide her concern.

"All will be well, auntie. I have Tarran and Lexi. But I don't know where George is?" Ava leaned closer to her aunt and whispered, "Do you think he's gone back to Fae?"

"No, no. He wouldn't leave you. He's been commanded by the King himself. He will be here."

"Train to Manchester Piccadilly now boarding on Platform Five," the announcement echoed around the station.

"Where is he?"

The quartet stared down the platform but saw nothing except the sweet trolleys being placed on board.

Lexi, Winifred and Ava searched for any sign of George amongst the hordes of people descending along the platform, but no sign of him.

A kerfuffle caught their attention. The crowds were ushered to one side leaving a path between them.

"Excuse me, excuse me, pardon me, excuse me. Oh, nice dress Madam! Excuse me, let me through. Thank you. Love the shoes! Thank you, excuse me."

The source of the voice came into view, a tall man with a turquoise velvet evening jacket, white slacks and suede brogues to match his jacket. He had blond hair, distinct features, a tiny nose which came not only to a point but sloped upwards. His skin was almost translucent, he glowed and glistened in the light. People stared, tutted and avoided him. The stranger skipped the last remaining steps to them.

"Not late, am I? Just can't be doing being late."

Ava squinted. "George?"

"It is I. I needed to be undercover, incognito."

"Couldn't you just have been invisible?"

"Oh no, where's the fun in that?" and George marched onto the train.

Ava shook her head and gave Aunt Winifred a hug.

"See you soon."

"Yes. Blessed be my darling."

George reached out his hand to Ava and helped her aboard. Tarran followed. Lexi and Winifred seemed to be communicating without words until Lexi said,

"Ever mind the rule of three. Follow this in mind and heart."

"Merry meet and merry part," replied Winifred.

The train moved and they waved farewell through the window.

After three changes and four delays, the quartet were finally on the train to Lincoln. Lexi had got through her chocolate stash by the time they pulled out of Bristol Temple Meads. Three hours later they were nearing Lincoln.

"I need chocolate. Where's the sweet trolley?" Lexi was fidgeting in her seat.

"You know auntie, you do eat an awful lot of chocolate."

"It's for energy, darling. Potency takes up so much of it, especially when you start to fly. I mean the number of calories you burn!"

"Not the answer you were looking for Ava?" asked George with his eyes still closed as he laid back on the seat.

George had begun to read Ava's mind and know her feelings long before she had a chance to know them herself.

"It's still all new to me, that's all. Will I fly? I'm a witch, aren't I?"

George opened his eyes and stared at Lexi who replied, "You're not a witch, Ava."

"But I thought I was. Haven't you all been telling me that?"

"No darling, not exactly. There's a long way to go before you become a witch. You may not even want to."

"I thought I had to?"

"It's a choice," said Tarran. "Just because you come from a certain heritage doesn't mean you have to follow it."

"It's all a choice darling," said Lexi. "We all have the freedom to choose what we want. And all I want right now is chocolate. I'm going to look for that sweet trolley."

"I'll go with you auntie. I need the loo. The toilets are just there. Don't worry, I'll be safe."

George nodded permission and Ava left.

The train rocked from side to side. It was difficult walking down the centre aisle so Ava held onto the head rests to steady herself. She would have apologised but there was no one in the carriage except the four of them. Aunt Lexi went through the automatic doors to the next carriage while Ava went to the bathroom. She turned to see Tarran and George at the far end and waved to them.

Locking the toilet door made the light come on, accompanied by an electrical humming.

"It's the light bulb. It needs changing," she said to herself as she washed her hands looking into the mirror. But the bulb was getting brighter, louder and crackled. Ava tingled all over as the hairs on her arms stood upright.

Quickly drying her hands, she pulled at the lock and fell out the bathroom door right on top of the sweet trolley. Straightening up, she saw the most beautiful bowl of fruit, including a bright red apple which placed on top of the oranges, bananas and pears. Ava could hardly take her eyes of it.

"Sorry," she murmured staring towards the steward, but there was something not quite right about him.

He had the same shine about him as George. His eyes had a purple tinge to them and his features were even more pronounced, more distinct, more angular. His white hair was tinged with purple spikes. He was as tall as George but not as gentle. In fact, there was nothing kind about this being in front of her. Fear griped her. She tried to move but he had wedged the trolley between her and the seats and she couldn't get around it.

She saw Tarran running towards her but the creature waved his hand and a ball of light plummeted down the carriage and hit Tarran. It exploded into a cage of water trapping Tarran inside.

He turned to Ava.

"Would you like some fruit, my sweet?"

From the corner of her eye, Ava saw George jump over the seats and fly towards her. It was all happening in slow motion, every heart beat felt like hours. Yet she could not take her eyes of the fruit. She could see her hand reaching out to the apple. She could feel her fingers touch it.

Time caught up with itself as a bolt of light sent the ball of fruit flying through the air. The apple splattered on the window which disintegrated as if eaten away by acid.

"Ava get behind me!" shouted George as he lifted the entire trolley, freeing her with a wave of his hand, sending it pinning the steward to the doors.

"George Wrenn. The King's loyal hand."

"Sir Robin Goodfellow."

"You can't protect her forever, Commander."

"I can today, my Lord," and George opened the doors. A rush of cold air drove Sir Robin Goodfellow and his trolley out of the speeding train.

George pressed the button to close the doors and wiped his hands together.

"Good riddance to bad rubbish," he said. "Not just a pretty face, eh!" and winked.

Aunt Lexi hurried into the carriage.

"What on earth?"

Tarran still stood like he'd taken a shower fully clothed. Ava ran to him.

"Tarran, are you alright?" she said over and over again.

"Yes, fine, I think. Who or what was that?" Tarran stared down the carriage towards Lexi and George, a broken window and a bowl of rotten fruit covered in maggots on the floor.

"That ladies and gentlemen, was Sir Robin Goodfellow, top agent for the enemy of Nothingness and General of the Army of Lost Souls. Have no fear Ava, we are on the side of truth."

Ava stood with her hand on her heart. She had a thousand questions but knew this wasn't the time and place. They were on a mission to get to the cathedral and find the next clue. She grabbed her pack back and the four silently left the train.

12. Robin Goodfellow

From every stormy wind that blows.
From every swelling tide of woes.
There is a calm, a safe retreat.
Tis found beneath the fairy seat.

After Tarran had changed into a dry set of clothes, the four set out on the long walk up to the cathedral which spread its shadow over Lincoln like a guardian angel. They didn't need to ask for directions. Up, up and up again. Steep Hill was true to its name and Ava sighed at the bottom of it.

"Too many people here George," said Aunt Lexi.

"Yes. It's impossible, unless a certain someone helps us. You do have the gift of time, Ava?"

"Do I?"

"Go on, good practice for you," encouraged Tarran.

"How?"

"Like you did on the train."

"I don't know what I did, everything just seemed to happen in slow motion, but it must have been in the blink of an eye."

"How did you feel just before you slowed time?" asked George.

"Frightened."

"Thought so, your gift is ruled by your emotions and more than likely, negative emotions."

"So, what do I do?"

"What do you feel looking at this hill?"

"Exhaustion."

George raised one of his eyebrows.

"Discouraged," said Ava.

"Right, hold onto that negative feeling and then imagine being at the top. How will that make you feel? Embrace the feelings, let emotion guide you."

Ava stared upwards. They had already faced danger on the

train and had walked from the station to get here. She could feel the heaviness in her heart pulling her down, everything slowed. People seemed to walk slower until they hardly moved. Within one breath lived a life time, a moment in time that Ava controlled.

"Hold my hand Tarran," Lexi told Tarran.

George did the same to Ava and all four flew swiftly upwards. At the top, time seemed to sort itself out and people started moving normally again. No-one around them noticed that at anything unusual had happened.

"Well done, Ava. Brilliant."

"Still not too sure how it actually works."

"All in good time," and off they marched towards the cathedral.

Tarran stepped aside and let Ava go in first.

"Always the gentleman Tarran, thank you."

The four stood in the entrance of the huge cathedral, its coolness welcoming.

In echoed steeped darkness shines the light from a Dean's Eye.

"Where is the Dean's Eye?"

"In the North transept. Here."

There were a few people milling about looking at the gothic architecture, especially the many gargoyles.

"The window was built between 1220 and 1235."

"Mmm," rose a collective not really bothered reply, so Tarran remained silent.

Nevertheless, it was impressive.

Checking that no one was looking, Lexi flew up to have a good look at the window. Ava watched, eyes wide open. Tarran kept a look out.

"Nothing out of the ordinary," said Lexi. "What does the rest of the verse say?"

Left from a Saint's shrine where pilgrim's meet for communion wine.

"Saint's shrine?"

"Where do people meet for Holy Communion?"

"At Saint Hugh's shrine," said Ava. "Here," she added, pointing. "Saint Hugh is often referred to as Saint Hugh of Avalon. He had a white swan who protected him and guarded him while he slept."

George and Lexi exchanged knowing looks.

"A white swan you say?" asked George.

"Yes, a beautiful one."

"Fancy that!" exclaimed Lexi, mysteriously.

"Here we are," said Ava as they reached the shrine. Opening her journal, she read the next couple of lines.

Follow the imp backwards in time where a Bishop sleeps, a direct line.

"The imp, the imp, where's the imp?"

"On the pillar," said Lexi, "there, just to the left, half way up. Do you see him?"

The three followed Aunt Lexi's extended arm upward.

"Nope, don't see it," replied Ava.

"There," said Tarran, pointing.

George checked no one was looking then appeared beside the imp, over twelve feet off the ground. He pointed to it.

"Now do you see it?" he laughed.

"George, get down! Yes, I do."

Lexi giggled as George fixed his velvet evening jacket while he floated back to the floor.

"Just trying to help," he replied.

"So, follow the imp backwards to where a Bishop sleeps."

Ava walked backwards towards the stone tomb of a sleeping man.

"This is the only one around," said Tarran

The symbol of a Tudor ship you will find.

Was there an image of a Tudor ship located at the crusader's resting place? Ava leaned against a small corner seat to look while the others searched up, down, left and right.

"We don't even know what we are looking for?" she said to herself, throwing her hands in the air and slumping back to the wall. Staring straight at her behind a small column was a piece of graffiti from centuries past - a Tudor ship.

Ava stared at it in disbelief, then pointed. Tarran saw her, called the others, and they joined her.

"Guys, I've found it!"

The three squeezed around to see. A beautiful Tudor ship was carved into the cream stone. It must have been detailed in its day but was now worn and chipped. The initials M. C. were carved near it, and the date.

"1735," said Lexi.

"Yes, what about it?"

"That was the year your ancestor built the house."

"So many coincidences," observed Tarran.

Lexi said, "This is more than chance, my friends. Much more. But it has been a long day. We need to rest. And I need to study a little. Besides, there are people coming. Let's leave and consider our next step. I know just where to go."

"Not all the way down that hill, is it auntie?"

"No darling, it's close by."

Aunt Lexi had had a shop in Lincoln all her life. Her mother had passed it to her but she rarely left the manor. She stayed most of the year at Candlesby. The shop was a true relic of the past, crooked and lopsided with books piled on the floor, dust everywhere. It was small and cramped and stacked floor to ceiling with knowledge. It had that fusty damp smell of ancient papers with a thousand stories to tell.

The door in the corner led upstairs to the first floor flat and its roof garden. The one-bedroom flat was small and filled with yet more books, but also plants, candles, scarves, chocolate - and mystery. It was yellow and white with illustrations of the moon, ancestral names, old photos and fading certificates dating back over a hundred years. A family's history on one wall of knowledge.

"Tarran," said Lexi in her most unwitchlike voice, "phone

for a pizza please. Ava, the bathroom and bedroom are there if you want a shower. Rummage around and wear what you like sweetie."

George decided to keep his human form for a while. For food, he was particularly attracted to the flowers and herbs on the roof garden.

"Those marigolds look particularly delicious," he said.

"Of course, help yourself. I'm off to check some books downstairs. Tarran, after you've ordered pizzas, come and join me. I've got something here that..." and off Aunt Lexi went, mumbling thoughts to herself.

Ava went to the bedroom, Tarran towards the phone and George ventured outside to the garden, busying himself creating a beautiful bowl of food.

Ava searched through the PJs and found a pair that would just about fit. The shelves around the bath were filled with aunt Lexi's homemade concoctions - bath bombs, lotions, oils, bottles galore of every shape and colour imaginable.

They each had handwritten labels - relaxing, calming, strengthening, vitality and enhance sleep, amongst many others. Ava felt exhausted. She ran the bath.

She loved a hot bath. Normally she feared water, but baths were different. They were not 'living' as she referred to streams, rivers and seas. There was something in living water that made her uneasy. She had learned to swim in a swimming pool. The instructor had told her father she was such a brilliant swimmer she could have been a mermaid. Yet the unease remained.

Running the bath water, Ava reached for Aunt Lexi's relaxing bath oil and a couple of handmade bath bombs. The heavy scent of lavender bubbles soothed her tired muscles and eased her active mind. So many thoughts swam round it and she fell asleep in the water, it was so calming. She heard the sweetest of voices like silk caressing the breeze.

"Wake up my darling. I'm so proud of you, but now you must wake. Wake up, Ava!"

She opened her eyes expecting to see Aunt Lexi or Aunt Winifred even, but nobody was the there. Reluctantly, she pulled the plug and allowed the soothing water to drain away.

She dressed and joined the others tucking into pizza.

"There you are! Enjoyed your bath? You've been in there for nearly an hour."

"What? I thought I'd only been a couple of minutes. I heard you call me, auntie."

"No darling, nobody called you."

"But I heard a voice, soft and beautiful."

"Perhaps it was the swan?" said Tarran.

George and Lexi gave him a hard stare.

"We've discovered some interesting information," said George. "Grab a chair and have some pizza before we eat it all. You must be starving. Make yourself comfy and we'll tell you what we've found."

13. The Code

The early June sun was gently setting over the medieval city as Ava settled down on of the huge cushions Lexi had in the garden. They sat in a circle drinking some kind of herbal tea concoction except for George who tucked into a bowl of flowers. Portions of pizza lay on a plate in the centre.

Each had their own pile of books, some old, some very old and some so ancient that their titles had completely disappeared from the covers. Taking a piece of cheesy pizza laden with vegetables, Ava asked, "So, what did you find out?"

"Many connections," said Tarran, "and all of them leading back to your family at Candlesby Manor."

"Your ancestor who built the manor in 1735 was a descendent of Sir Francis Drake," added Lexi.

"I never knew that. Dad didn't tell me."

"There's a lot your father didn't tell you, but all in good time," mumbled George.

"Sir Francis Drake," said Tarran, "circumnavigated the world between 1577 and 1580 was knighted by Queen Elizabeth I on his famous ship, the Golden Hind."

"There was a picture of her in the great Corridor of Colour. You said she was one of the few human monarchs who knew about the Fae."

The flower petals were bulging George's cheeks.

"I did. And she did. I say, these petals are scrumptious."

"Tell her about the ship," said Lexi, eating even more quickly than before. The more excited they got about relaying information, the more Lexi and George ate. Only Tarran refrained - knowledge was his meal.

"The Tudor ship is one of your family symbols, a hidden code that only your family understand."

"I don't understand anything," and Ava slumped back on the cushion. "Where is the treasure? Where does this all this lead?"

George said, "The Horn of Bran. It was part of the inventory log on the Golden Hind."

"We have an inventory of a Tudor pirate ship?"

"A-hem, it was no pirate ship and Sir Francis Drake was no pirate. Yes, we do have a record of the inventory. Surprising what I have in this shop," Aunt Lexi replied, tapping a faded book beside her.

"Ok, but where do we find it? And what's so special about this Horn of Bran?"

"We are not too sure where it is, but we do think we need to visit the ship."

"The ship still exists?"

"A replica does in London, in St. Mary's Dock actually. I think we might find another clue there or at least a little more about the ship."

"She wasn't just the first ship to sail round the world but also the first ship to sail around worlds."

"What do you mean Aunt Lexi?"

"We mean, darling, she was able to sail to other realms, such as Fae, collect the Horn as a gift for Queen Elizabeth."

It took a few moments for this to sink in.

"This is an unexpected turn of events," said Ava. "I didn't think the task was going to be easy but I didn't think it would be this complicated."

"It is part of the Codex, Ava," said George.

Lexi got up to light the candles as night drew in around them.

"The Codex?"

"The Fairy Codex. As part of your education, it is my duty to explain it to you. There are five rules:

1: Nature can be friend or foe
2: Be prepared for the unknown
3: Chaos can be hidden order
4: Within darkness there is light
5: Tidiness leads to fairy-ness"

"Mmm," said Ava, "I can understand the chaos bit, that's

60

similar to the chaos theory."

George waved his hand dismissively.

"Don't try to understand this Master in your scientific, methodical way. This is Fae, this is the Other."

"What other?"

"All in good time. There is much we must take from this day. We know the first treasure is the Horn of Bran. You are connected to it somehow, Ava. We also know Robin Goodfellow is on to you."

Finally!

"Who is he?"

"He started out as a member of King Ostar and Queen Amber's court. In the last dynasty of the Age of Dragon, King Ostar and Queen Amber were a stunning couple. Their portraits can be seen all over the world. Many fairy houses to this day have pictures and paintings of these monarchs…"

"The Age of Dragon?"

"You need to read your father's book," tutted Lexi.

George continued, "Robin Goodfellow was a shape shifter extraordinaire, able to transform himself into the epitome of beauty, and was welcomed at court. However, Sir Robin Goodfellow has always been an agent of the Dark - the Nothingness, the emptiness. He is often thought of as goblin or demon but has many guises. He is known as Puck, the Welsh call him Pwca, pronounced the same as his Irish incarnation, the Pooka.

"In his guise as the Pooka, he can appear as a black horse or black dog. He is known for taking life. In other words, similar to the Banshee, he is a harbinger of death. Yet despite this, there is a mesmerising quality about him which draws human and Fae alike. Do you realise the grave danger you were in, Ava? Do you realise how close he came? We can't afford to be complacent, not for a moment."

Lexi returned from a brief trip downstairs with a book in hand.

"Here Ava, I have the proof copy of your father's published book, The Hieroglyphic Fae: The Sacred Language of Fairies by Professor R.G. Fellow."

Handing the book over, Ava gently caressed it.

"I haven't seen the printed version before."

All was quiet as she flicked through pages in the soft glow of the candles. She read the inscription:

Dedicated to Ava...
Do not follow me on this path.

The stars were twinkling as if winking to Ava. She took a deep breath of the night air and filled her lungs.

14. Nature

Lexi had changed the return journey enabling them to visit London. Although the Golden Hind was a replica, they felt they had to see it and go on board. The train journey would take them through to St Pancras via Cambridgeshire.

"Have we any idea what we are looking for?"

"None whatsoever," said George, pulling his green and white Fedora over his eyes. "but we will know it when we find it."

He had changed again, this time to bright green skinny jeans and a loose white shirt with a striped waistcoat that draped long at the back like a mermaid's tail. George maintained a distinctive style, definitely a major trend setter of the Avalonian wave.

The train jilted forward and was soon whizzing through the countryside. Tarran had his nose buried deep in an historical tome from Lexi's shop.

"What's it about Tarran?" Ava asked.

"The Thirteen Treasures. Fascinating stuff."

Ava starred out the window, restless. Even Aunt Lexi had stopped nibbling chocolate and was dozing. She opened her father's book, The Hieroglyphic Fae and read the inscription again.

Dedicated to Ava...
Do not follow me on this path.

She read the contents page:

What are Faeroglyphs?
The Fairy Scribe
Timeline of Fae Ages
Royal Houses
Body and Wings.

A lump caught in her throat and it was hard to swallow. The events of the past couple of days had made her forget how much she missed him. He was all she had. Ava had never known her mother. They said she had died when Ava was born and the loss was great that her father could never speak of it. Ava never questioned him, he would close up immediately if she so much as mentioned her mother. Ava didn't even know her name.

The train screeched forward jilting George and Lexi back, Ava and Tarran forward. The conductor ran down the carriage towards the driver. Startled passengers listened to the announcement.

"Hello, this is your driver speaking. I'm afraid there is an obstruction on the tracks. We're being held here until it is moved. Apologies for any inconvenience caused."

A mumbled dismay of disgruntled passengers was heard.

"We can't wait here, who knows how long it's going to be?" said Tarran, picking up his book from the floor.

"We'll miss the opening hours at the Golden Hind and our connection home," Lexi added.

"Come on, let's go," replied George straightening his waistcoat and putting his hat firmly on.

It is not an easy thing to open a train door at the wrong time in the wrong place, and the conductor did not like it.

"I'm sorry sir, what are you doing?"

"How far are we from Stevenage?"

"Half a mile but you…"

"Right then, we are fly…"

"…walking, he meant walking. We walk very fast, almost like flying. Thank you. Bye," explained Lexi as she whisked the door open and jumped off the train, something which should not have been possible, let alone legal.

Tarran tapped the open-mouthed conductor on the shoulder. "Which way?"

"Er…over there, sir, through those fields."

"Thank you," and out jumped Tarran, followed by Ava, helped by George.

"Nice day for a walk," added Lexi as the four headed through a muddy field. The wheat was almost ready to be harvested, just a couple more weeks of sunshine and it would be perfect.

"We are still in view George," said Lexi, "we can't fly yet."

"Over that hill, they won't be able to see us on the other side."

George and Tarran raced each other, but Lexi wobbled slowly and Ava couldn't keep up, her legs felt leaden. She could see Tarran beating George to the hill and Lexi behind, laughing. Ava stretched her arms out as she caressed the wheat with her fingers. A cloudless blue sky overhead and a gentle breeze swept through the field.

From the corner of one eye she saw a scarecrow, large with purple flecks surrounding him. She carried on walking towards the others who were all on top of the hill.

A noise.

She stopped, it stopped.

The scarecrow was some way away, but now directly behind her. Ava was sure it had been to the left of her, but maybe not.

Carrying on walking, the sound resumed.

Ava quickened her pace, so did the echo, rustling, rustling, closer and closer.

She sprinted faster as the fear cut deeper.

Huge wings flapped round her and an icy blast swept through the field knocking her down.

She fell with a thud.

No sooner had her head hit the ground than the scarecrow was hovering over her with its hideous features, wings like an outstretched dragon, purple veins pulsating through them. Its eyes were purple and narrow, its black mouth clicking and making strange sounds. Dazed and confused she willed herself to speak. Hardly moving her lips, she muttered the terrible name, "Robin Goodfellow."

An almighty screech escaped the hideous mouth. It was the sound she had heard that night. Darkness encased her as other shadowy figures approached. Tarran and George! They reached her, Lexi followed, pulling on the wheat as she raced along, weaving the wheat stalks into a pentacle, chanting as she ran:

Hear now words of the wise.
Our course unseen through heaven's eyes.
Come to me ancient power,
Fairy magic upon this hour.

As the last word fell from her lips she threw the pentacle to the ground, exploding into purple smoke.

The scarecrow melted. Its thin straw fingers clawed their way towards Ava but they could not reach her.

"Ava, Ava! She's not waking up!" Tarran cried.

"Wait," whispered George.

Out of a clear sky, something appeared. A tiny cloud, shiddering as if being rung by a pair of giant hands.

At once, it started to rain, not water but flowers of such heady scents and bright colours - lavender, hyacinths, lilac, daisies and sunflower petals. They fell to Earth in an iridescent rainbow.

Ava woke. Opening her eyes, she saw her friends peering at her, flowers and petals in their hair. Their faces and clothes glittered with sparkling colours.

"The Cloud of Believing!" Ava whispered as the flowers fell. And in amongst them appeared the Fairy Queen herself, gently floating down upon a sheaf of lavender.

George bowed his head and stepped away. Lexi curtseyed and moved away also. Tarran stayed by Ava's side, holding her hand.

The Queen stepped from the lavender and glided over to them. She held her tiny hand over Ava's forehead who could feel her strength pouring back.

"Your Majesty, I thought you only appeared in Avalonia."

"Avalonia is everywhere in nature. You are never far away from us. You are more a part of us than you will ever know child. We will try to protect you, but you must be careful. All of you must be careful. The King and I will not always be free to protect you. Do you understand? Do you all understand? I hope so. I truly do. But now you must continue your journey."

Ava staggered to her feet.

"Where is Robin Goodfellow? Is he gone?"

"For now. Only when the enemy is defeated can we be truly free of him. Hurry now. Your train leaves soon and there is so much for you to do."

A shadow swooped towards them, but it was not Goodfellow, it was a crow with piercing eyes that studied them all and winked at George. It bowed to the Queen who climbed onto a wing whereupon the crow rose high into the clear sky with the Cloud of Believing behind.

"You heard her majesty," said George, "we'd better get a move on if we want to make that train."

"Are you alright?" Tarran asked Ava. "That was close. Again."

"Yes, thank you. Let's go," and with that she led the race to the station, Lexi holding her as they flew over fields and paths and stiles and farmsteads.

The Golden Hind was a beautiful ship, elegant, detailed and proud. Tarran was already the tour guide.

"It was originally called the Pelican but was renamed by Drake in honour of his patron Sir Christopher Hatton, whose crest was the golden hind. A female red deer.

"The red deer is also a symbol of the Fae. Is that not true George?" Ava asked. Her studies of her father's book were paying off.

"Everything in nature is Fae in some form," he said, perhaps a touch sharply.

"Everything in nature is to be respected," said Lexi, "and has deeper meaning."

Ava heard the authority in both George's and Lexi's voices which hadn't been there before. Even Tarran was quiet.

The four explored different parts of the ship. Ava ventured down into the galley, alone. This might have seemed risky but she was safe enough - Robin Goodfellow would need time to regain his strength after Lexi's powerful spell.

The wooden deck creaked. Ava stood alone in the centre within the dark womb of the ancient ship. Closing her eyes, she asked herself, 'What was it truly like then? What happened here?'

Her breathing slowed. She felt warm, surrounded by swirling mists of time. Her skin tingled and a smell of candles and wood drifted through the air. She could hear heavy footsteps above and the ship swayed from side to side.

Opening her eyes, she saw none other than Queen Elizabeth the First and a man kneeling at her feet, holding a large drinking horn with a silver engraved base. The Queen was speaking but Ava heard nothing.

"Let me hear. Please?" Ava had no idea who she was asking but she stepped closer to the scene and listened. Sure enough, the words became audible, soft and first, then louder.

"Our enemies are close Sir Francis, we must protect the innocent. Hide the Horn of Bran on the Holy Island."

"I will do as you command, Ma'am. May God protect you and the realm."

Raising her head, the Queen stared straight into Ava's eyes. "May God protect us all," and she nodded to Ava as the tableau dissolved.

It was a brief but telling scene. When it faded, Ava stood alone once more in the dark.

15. Bran

Bran Galed brin y gelwynt
Bonedd Gwyr y Gogledd gynt
Taliesin, ddewn ddiwael
A'I troes yn well n'or Tri Hael

Niggardly Bran they used to call him
Of old was descended from the Nobility of the North
Taliesin, no mean magician
Transformed him into one better than the Tri Hael
(Guto'r Glyn)

Candlesby Manor was a welcome sight for the four quest seekers. It appeared in darkness through the trees but as Ava approached, she could see lights on the ground floor. Aunt Holly and Aunt Meadow stood in the doorway. Meadow's arms encased Tarran and Holly wrapped hers round Ava.

"I've missed you two and you've only been gone a couple of days. The house has never been so quiet."

"What did you find out?" Meadow asked.

The story of their encounters tumbled out excitedly. Robin Goodfellow, the Horn of Bran, Holy Island…. Ava wanted to tell everything in a moment. Holly and Meadow listened, appalled at the danger and what it all meant.

"Come inside," said Meadow. "We made a good wholesome stew. Then bath and bed. You can tell us more in the morning."

Their heavy feet fell flat on the stone hall floor. They were exhausted. A welcome tap, tap, tap cheered them a little.

"Hello Jennifer!" Ava wearily ruffled Jennifer's curly hair.

The events of the past couple of day had definitely taken its toll. Flying, shape-shifting and manipulating time were exhausting, so for breakfast next morning Ava found herself tucking into the chocolate basket.

"A-ha! Caught you! Knew it would catch up with you soon enough."

George flew in, back to his usual fairy self. The aunts entered the breakfast room one by one and immediately started to rummage through the chocolate basket. George winked at Ava.

"Was it a nice night for flying ladies?"

Looking like they had been caught out, Lexi responded with, "Of course. We had to do a perimeter protection for the estate just in case."

"Why?" Asked Tarran entering with a trayful of toast, sausages, eggs, bacon and beans.

The aunts' eyes widened as they each grabbed plates and sat down whilst sharing out serving dishes of the superb English breakfast Tarran had cooked up.

"I know how important breakfast is when you've got a full day of work ahead," he said.

"Most important meal of the day," Ava added, eyeing the food hungrily.

They ate their full, and then a little more, not speaking too much, saving their energy for whatever was to happen next.

Afterwards, they headed into the library. Staring at the flip chart with the first clue still written on it, Ava said, "The place doesn't feel the same without Aunt Winifred."

"We're a coven without its High Priestess, and so near Midsummer!" said Holly.

"High Priestess?"

Holly looked as though she had said something she shouldn't have.

"It's alright Holly," Lexi reassured her, "Ava knows who and what we are."

George had decided to sit in Winifred's chair which seemed bigger with a fairy sitting in it. He punched and kicked the cushion until finally flopping into it as it folded round him. He gave a contented sigh.

"Right, so what do we know so far?" Lexi asked, turning the flip chart paper over.

"The Horn of Bran is on the Holy Island."

"And where is the Holy Island?"

Silence. Everyone thinking intensely. Even George did his best impression of thinking, at least the best a fairy could do.

Tarran said, "There is one obvious place it could be." They waited for him to continue. "Lindisfarne," he told them.

"Ah, yes, Lindisfarne," and Lexi wrote the name down. "Which is where, exactly?"

Tarran already had the answer.

"Northumberland, postal town - Berwick upon Tweed."

"Wow Tarran! Just wow!" Ava exclaimed, impressed.

They were all impressed. And Tarran had even more to say.

"It's not easy to reach. It's cut off by a tidal causeway so we have to check the crossing times. I assume we won't go by train, not after last time?"

They agreed. It was too much of a risk with Robin Goodfellow following their every move.

"What do we know about Lindisfarne?" Lexi asked. "And what do we know about Bran?"

"Anything in The Book of Shadows?" asked Meadow. "It's your family book, Ava," she added, explaining.

"It's worth a try," Lexi said.

"But no-one can get in unless Winnie is here."

"Or a High Priestess."

Ava once again felt like the whole world knew what was going on except her.

"Hello, I'm still in the room," and she waved her hand.

"Shall we?"

"I don't think Winnie would mind, plus it is her heritage."

"Am I invisible?"

"I don't know… are you? Have you projected yet?"

"What?"

"Ladies," said George, "we are wandering off the path, and although Ava can manipulate time, it still ticks on. Come on Ava, you must see the clock tower."

Tarran was at the library door before her.

"Well," he said, "haven't you ever wondered? I'm dying to know what's in there."

"Not really. Grandma closed it off after the great storm.

Even Aunt Winifred and Dad never went in there."

"Or did they?" said Lexi, raising her eyebrows.

"Come on," Tarran pulled at Ava. "They'll get there before us."

"It won't make any difference," said George, "they won't be able to get in. Only one who possesses special abilities can open the door and unlock the book."

The aunts were there, huddled around the door expectantly, waiting. It was a tiny door, so small that only one person could fit through it at a time, sideways, and bowing their head. Even then, Tarran would find it difficult.

Holly and Meadow moved back a couple of stairs to let Ava through. She was the one. Despite her lack of experience, no one else could do what had to be done.

"Go on Ava, try, see if it opens."

Lexi's eyes were as wide as saucers. It was Christmas Day to her.

Ava reached out her hand, then stopped.

"Are there any words I need to say?"

"We don't think so. Try."

Ava reached out her hand again, her fingers almost touching the blue and white porcelain handle.

"What happens if it doesn't let me in?"

"Don't think negative thoughts."

"I won't be turned into a frog or anything will I?"

"We'll put you in a nice pond if it happens," said George.

Ava saw how much they needed her and couldn't let them down. She grabbed the handle, twisted it, turned it, pushed it, pulled it.

Nothing. A sigh of disappointment echoed through the tiny space.

Just for a moment.

Then the door clicked, creaked and slowly opened.

16. The Clocktower

Ava peeped round the door slowly. "Oh my!"

"What do you see?"

"Wonderous things!"

The tiny door disguised the sheer size of the clocktower. After crouching sideways to get in, Lexi opened her arms in admiration. Holly and Meadow followed.

Ava gazed round the huge room, lit by numerous windows and a skylight with a stained-glass window depicting a Tudor ship shining reds, pinks, yellows, blues and greens on the floor.

Two hideous gargoyles guarded the door, their features almost real, yet inhuman. They had pointy ears and almond shaped eyes, more Elfin than Fae.

The space inside was the size of Candlesby Manor. Shelves galore adorned every wall from floor to ceiling, herbs hung on some of the beams whilst dried varieties were already stored in hundreds of jars labelled alphabetically. Jars of spices, bottles of potions, rows of books, measuring cups, weights, rulers, feather quills, plants and medieval weapons, a bow and arrow, an axe and a glowing suit of armour – the room was beating with a dazzling, mystical heart.

"Fairy wings, poisoned dragon's liver, dragon's blood, mermaid tears, unicorn horn shavings," Ava read.

"Yes, yes, yes," said George, "let's not discuss those now, shall we? Let's get to the book. You never know when a place like this will chuck you out. Doesn't appreciate it's time being wasted, you know. Tick tock, after all."

The book stood on its own lectern in the centre, its holy place. The aunts stood round it as Ava approached with Tarran beside her. He said, "The book has a wealth of knowledge. It is said to have been written by the first victim of the witch trials in the world, Petronilla de Meath. Only her direct descendants are able to open the book once it has been sealed by the High Priestess. Imposters will be turned to stone."

"Tarran!" Meadow scolded.

"That's what I read! Ava is no imposter."

"Go on Ava, ignore him, see if it opens."

"How?"

"To you it's a normal book, but to us its locked. Look…"

Holly tried opening it, but even though it had no lock or seal, it would not open.

"It's protected. Even though we are all witches, only those who possess a certain purity can open it."

Lexi said, "Go on Ava, we know you can do it."

Ava glanced at George.

"Show 'em what you got, Princess."

Ava touched the book and the invisible seal in the shape of a triquetra opened into three circles. The triquetra glowed gold upon the black leather book, looking like it was made of water, not leather. It rippled and breathed like the sea. The book opened.

There was a general sigh of relief and admiration.

"Princess," muttered George.

There was no index or contents page and as Ava flicked through it she could see different forms of handwriting. It had been written over centuries by her ancestors. As she searched for some form of reference page her eyes fell upon an inscription in the front:

> *A child of prophecy shall appear,*
> *A child of grace the enemy will fear.*
> *Born of human and divine,*
> *Her gifts shall include time.*
> *She shall have powers three*
> *And command realms both human and fairy.*

"Yes, well, let's move on, shall we?"

"George, this sounds awfully like m…"

Ava was engrossed in the book. It drew her in and told her what she needed to know.

She whispered to the others, "It is said that whatever you wish for to drink shall appear in the Horn of Bran."

"Oh, how delicious! A never-ending supply of Chardonnay."

Ava gently turned the pages, totally focused. The book was full of spells, descriptions of supernatural beings, recipes on potions, health, the natural world and even the heavens beyond Earth. She read aloud where the book told her to read aloud, from a decorative page complete with dragons:

> *In the year of Our Lord 793, the Anglo-Saxon chronicle recorded:*
> *'In this year fierce, foreboding omens came over the land of the Northumbrians, and the wretched people shook, there were excessive whirlwinds, lightning and fiery dragons were seen flying in the sky. These signs were followed by great famine, and a little after those, that same year on 6th Ides of January, the ravaging of wretched heathen men destroyed God's church at Lindisfarne.'*

She added, "Here's a footnote, C.F. Elizabeth I. And more:"

> *Lindisfarne Castle had considerable work carried out during Queen Elizabeth's reign in 1565. Strengthening the fort and providing gun platforms for the developments in artillery technology. One of the crossbows can be found in the war cabinet.*

"I think these are the items in question," said George who had opened a likely lopoking massive wooden cabinet.

"Wow!"

"Oh, wow indeed!" replied Ava.

Inside was a huge collection of ancient, medieval weaponry.

"Just look at this," Tarran said turning to his mother, holding a seven headed axe.

"Let's not get ahead of ourselves," Meadow replied, gently taking the axe from Tarran's hands and placing it back in the cabinet.

"Let's take the book downstairs and continue in the library

shall we?" said Aunt Lexi.

"I thought only I could touch the book?" said Ava.

"Only a member of the ancient bloodline can open it but anyone the book trusts can hold it."

"And the door?"

"The room will remain unlocked while the book is away and close when it is returned. It will then be sealed till the next time its needed."

Ava had so many questions but she glanced round the room as the others made their way downstairs and spoke to it.

"You let me in, you let me read. Thank you. I'm going now, but I want to spend a lot of time in here, if you'll let me."

For once in her life, she felt like she was home.

The stone gargoyles shifted ever so slightly as they whispered in unison, "Ava."

17. The Professor

As the aunts settled back down in the library with their piles of books, Jennifer sidled up to Ava, wagging her tail. She was desperate to read more from the Book of Shadows, but Jennifer was even more desperate for a walk.

"I won't be long," she said.

"I'll go with you," Tarran offered.

"No, it's alright, you stay and study."

Ava gently placed the Book of Shadows on Tarran's knees. His eyes sparkled.

"I'll go with you instead," said George.

"No, really, it's alright George. I'll stay in sight of the house."

"I have to, remember?"

She remembered the King's command, and the moments since when they'd left her alone, supposedly safe. It was not that Ava didn't want George's company, she just wanted some alone time, or at least Jennifer time.

"I need to gather supplies from the garden," George insisted.

"Supplies?"

"You'll see."

Jennifer pulled at the lead as she investigated every flower, smelling one, then another. George flitted from herb to herb to flower to flower. He sang as he roamed:

> Plant rosemary by your garden gate.
> Lavender for luck.
> Fennel for your weight.
> Mint for health and basil for wealth.
> Many use sage and thyme.
> Feverfew gives piece of mind.

"There's so much I don't know, George. How can I learn a

lifetime's knowledge in a matter of weeks?"

"Knowledge is concentric circles, ever expanding. A little today becomes greater tomorrow, like throwing a stone into a pond and watching the ripples flow ever outward."

Ava breathed in the air. The gentle summer breeze was refreshing. She listened to the trees and George watched her.

"Do you hear their song?" he asked.

"Not quite."

"In time. Trees are allies of ours and they are also healers. We need the old apple tree. Come on."

"Wait up, George. Jennifer, this way," and Ava gave a gentle tug on Jennifer's lead.

The old apple tree stood alone from the others. Its branches were withered and its leaves were scraggy. The apples that formed on it were rotten. Ava had been warned repeatedly never to eat from this tree.

"There's no apples at the moment, George, and even if there were, we are not meant to eat them."

"Its not the apples we need, Princess, it's the bark."

George lighted on the trunk, knocked three times and bowed his head.

"With your permission my Lady, may I have some bark for our journey?"

The tree creaked and moved slightly, but not from the breeze. Something was moving within. The huge knot on the trunk took form. Jennifer barked and stood wagging her tail expectantly.

"Shush," soothed Ava, bending down to ruffle Jennifer's hair.

When she stood back up, she saw a face peering from the trunk. It had kindly features touched by the passages of time.

"Hello. And hello to you too, Jennifer. Oh, young Master George Wrenn, how's you this fair day? Dear Ava, come closer child, my old eyes are not what they used to be, and I do go back somewhat. From Pagan times, you know. Long years past."

"Hello, Lady … Apple Tree?" said Ava, trying to be polite.

The face giggled.

"How courteous she is? Call me Grandmother Apple my

dear, for I have known you since before you were born."

"You have?"

"Oh yes. Now, how can I help you?"

George spoke.

"Lady, may we have bark for the journey. We may have use of your healing powers."

"Of course. And you Ava, what would you like most?"

"There is something I would like Grandmother Apple, and that is to see my father and know that he is alright."

"Cut one of my apples in half Ava, you will see a pentagram inside. Stand in front of a mirror at midnight, hold the apple by the light of a blue candle and you will see your father."

"There is no fruit on the tree, Grandmother."

"Reach for the branch," Grandmother Apple yawned and stretched her branches until one touched Ava.

A petal blossomed, then blew away. A tiny apple formed which grew, reddened and was ready to pick. Four seasons in one day, three seasons in a breath. As she picked the fruit, a sharp breeze swept round them.

"What about the Nothingness? What about the darkness that holds my father prisoner?"

"Yes, the enemy. Know this - where hearts are empty and minds have no dreams, the Nothingness gains strength. But you are a child of grace. You are full of love. Never fear the Nothingness for you are everything and it cannot compete with you. Only self-doubt and sadness will allow it to destroy you. Believe in yourself. Believe in your power. Sweet dreams my child, good morrow Master Wrenn."

George bowed his head and dipped his wings as Grandmother Apple disappeared into the tree.

"Will I really be able to see my father, George?"

"She told you so, and she is as wise as she is old."

"How old?"

"She was here long before your ancestor built the house. Some say it was her who advised them to build it here."

"And how old are you Commander Wrenn? She called you young?"

George ruffled his yellow cravat.

"You should never ask a gentleman how old they are. However, just this once. I am 27."

"Well, that's not really old."

"Twenty seven thousand."

"Days? Weeks? Months?"

"Years."

It took Ava a moment to digest this, so George continued, "I have seen many sights and fought in many battles, but the one we are now facing is the most dangerous I have ever known. This is the one that will change everything."

His last words were melancholy. His wings lowered and he slowly drifted to the ground. Ava reached out her hand to him.

"George, remember, we have right on our side."

Springing back up again, he said, "Yes. Yes… you are wise beyond your years, Ava. Now, you remember how to use that?" he said, pointing to the apple.

"Yes, cut it halfway."

"Halfway, sideways like this, straight through the middle and you see the pentagram."

"Yes, will do."

Night couldn't come quick enough. She prepared everything in silence. She didn't want the aunts to know and she didn't want Tarran to know either for that matter. She knew he would want to stay and watch what happens and she needed to do this alone. It was bad enough with George hovering outside her room all night. Besides, the aunts would be doing their perimeter sweeps of the estate.

A little after dark, she cut the apple and, after lighting the candle, stood in front of the mirror with the pentagram reflected.

Nothing!

Absolutely nothing.

Jennifer, curled up on her bed, opened one eye.

"Nothing, Jen."

Jennifer closed her eye and covered her face with a paw.

"You're right, it's too light, it needs to be darker… by candle light alone, that's what Grandmother Apple meant."

The candle flame flickered. Dancing shadows played across the wall as Jennifer yawned and lay flat out, dog style. In the mirror Ava appeard to be back in her shorts and T-shirt, her curly hair tied back in a ponytail.

The candle was now the only light. Standing in front of the mirror with blackness surrounding her, the candle flame made her reflection flicker. She closed her eyes and imagined her father. 'Dad are you alright? Please, let me see him tonight.' She hoped the rhyme might prove to be her first spell. She took a deep breath and opened her eyes.

Nothing but her own reflection.

She lowered her gaze to the floor. Such a heavy feeling weighed upon her. Almost despairing, she looked again into the mirror.

Nothing.

Except…

The peculiar blue light of the flame, and within the flame she glimped her father.

"Dad?"

"For a moment, yes, it's me."

"Dad! I have a hundred questions. Are you alive? That's the most important one. Are you?"

"Ava I can't be long. I won't be able to stay but know that I'm alright and I'm so sorry I didn't tell you everything. I thought we had more time."

"It's ok. I've been to Fae! Yes, I have! George Wrenn is with me.We can help, I'm sure. Where are you being held prisoner?"

"No Ava, it's too dangerous. The Entity will trap you."

"It already tried… twice, with Robin Goodfellow."

"He was the one that imprisoned me here. Be on your guard. He can appear as anything or anyone. And be careful of the descendants of the Blue Men."

"Blue Men?"

"The Mer people."

"I will, I promise. Dad, you must tell me, where are you being held?"

"The Castle of Glass. It is not as it sounds, Ava, not bright, not clear, not beautiful. Evil has mastered it and all the sorrow and sadness has shattered the light. It is dark, cold and empty. I am imprisoned in a terrible emptiness. Whatever controls it feeds on fear so if I show fear, it grows stronger, and I fear for you, my daughter, not for myself."

The flickering flame of her father faded.

"Dad, don't go."

"I can't stay Ava, it's pulling me back. I cannot stay."

"Can I see you again? Dad? Please don't go!"

No answer.

Whatever power commanded her father, it was too strong to deny, at least for now. Professor Riley was gone. Ava stood alone, the candle flickering down to the last millimetre of wax. The apple had worn paper thin and as she moved her fingers around it, it broke into pieces and floated away like feathers of light.

They glistened as they disappeared.

18. The Journey North

Never before has such terror appeared in Britain as we have suffered from a pagan race. The heathens poured out the blood of saints around the altar and trampled on their bodies in the temple of God, like dung in the streets.
(Alcuin, a Northumbrian scholar in Charlemagne's Court.)

After breakfast, Ava burst into her bedroom and grabbed her rucksack. She tipped it upside down and emptied everything on the bed. 'It must be clean and tidy before I start packing,' she told herself.

A varied collection of sweet wrappers, chewing gum, plasters and train tickets filed through her hands. 'The plasters I'll keep, just in case.' Putting them to one side, she paused at the train ticket, holding it at the corner for a closer read.

Had it really only been two weeks since she arrived here?

Had it just been two weeks since her father's disappearance? And look what she had learned in that time - a world witnessed only by a chosen few

She feared her destiny. She did not want this task, but it was the only way to bring the Son of Prophecy back and free her father.

Decisively, she tossed the ticket into the bin. It was a return ticket, but she would never be returning home, not that way, at least. Too much had changed - she had changed. She was no longer lonely and afraid. There was something inside her, a power that had been released. She had a world to defend.

'What do I need?' she asked herself. 'Where am I going? My journey is north but that is all I know.' She flopped onto the bed and sat, shaking her head. 'Dad help me, what do I need?'

A gentle breeze from the open window carried the scent of honeysuckle and elder blossom. She had known that smell before. Ava opened her eyes and reached for her notebook and pen. 'We always need to keep records, Dad. We need our journal, don't we?'

Grabbing her purse, she threw that in the rucksack along with plasters, a purse, a pen and the field journal. Everything else she needed was inside her. She was ready.

It was early morning as Lexi drove the 1958 Wolseley Riley round to the front of the manor. Ava thought it funny that a car should be the inspiration for her father's name. Her Grandmother had a wicked sense of humour, naming her father after the bottle-shaped car painted two shades of green. At least they would travel in style.

Tarran sat in front as the self-appointed map reader. George had chosen to change again. Instead of 1960s he now dressed in a 1920s style green tweed jacket and yellow tartan waistcoat with trousers ending at the knees. He wore brown and green Argyll socks, soft suede laced Oxfords and a Panama hat.

"I hope we don't have to stop anywhere," said Ava. "Are you intending to wear that all the way to Lindisfarne?"

"I see we are still in our night clothes," George replied.

"Fresh on this morning. It's my best T-shirt and these shorts are new."

George sighed. The young had no taste.

"Can we all get in please," Lexi told them. "We have a long way to go, and in case you've all forgotten, Midsummer is in three days. Just three days."

Lexi gave two honks of the horn and the car pulled away.

Ava turned back to Candlesby Manor and waved to her aunts. Staring at the madness and majesty of the manor, she whispered to herself, 'What a fascinating house and family I come from!'

The journey was to take about six hours. Ava got comfy and was just about to close her eyes when George nudged her and held out her father's book.

"No time for sleep, Princess. Let's begin that education of yours. Go to the section, 'Timeline of Fae Ages'. Let's start at the beginning. Isn't that the logical place to begin?"

Resistance was futile. She read about the First Age of

Avalonia, how human and fairies evolved, how they went their own ways, the battles fought, the learning, the lessons, the famous and the not so famous.

"The golden bluebell?" she said aloud at an interesting point in the chapter.

"A truly magnificent flower," George explained, "picked to extinction in the Age of Unicorn."

"We still have some back at the Manor," said Lexi from the driver's seat. "You'll have to look when we return. A most beautiful smell as I recall."

There was so much in the book, almost as many questions as answers.

"Did a Will o' the Wisp bury the thirteen treasures?" she asked.

Lexi peered at George through the mirror.

"It's a possibility," said George. "We never thought of that, did we Lexi? We assumed it was humans, but that makes sense. After all, it is what Will o' the Wisps are notorious for. I shall send my shadow to investigate."

"Your shadow?"

"I can only send my shadow separately when I am in human form. When I am in my natural state, fae don't have shadows. Watch."

George pulled at his hand until a black shape emerged which grew until it was human size, sitting between him and Ava.

"Right," said George, "you heard what was said, off you go and see what you can find out. There must be someone with knowledge of this. Go now and seek the truth."

George's shadow gave a slight acknowledgement, jumped out the car and disappeared onto the black tarmac.

"Where's he gone?" Tarran asked.

"Slipped into an In-Between, places that can become doorways into Fae. Crossroads where at least two roads meet create doorways to other places. The same with paths, rivers, streams – converging - not quite here and not quite there. Doorways also are In-Betweens, as are certain roundabouts like the one we've just passed, Black Cat. Time, too, like the moment between night and day - midnight. It could be that there are more In-Betweens than actual Here-I-Ams! That's a joke, Ava," he said, when he saw her puzzled expression. "What is not a joke is the hour between 12.00 pm and 1.00 am.It is the most dangerous time."

"The witching hour," Lexi interrupted.

"Yes, when the battle begins between good and evil. Both have equal rights to the hour. The wicked use it for all manner of beastly things whilst…"

"…we good witches protect the world, healing the rifts and guard the doorways the best way we can."

"Which is how?"

"Spells and rituals. Usually at the Heart of the Forest."

Round the stones, three times three, energy and healing we bring to thee, Goddess of day and Goddess of night, grant us strength to do what's right. For love and light grant this to me, an it harm none so mote it be.

As Lexi chanted the spell, she tapped on the steering wheel every syllable and after she'd finished she gave a little giggle.

George was not amused and instead raised one eyebrow.

"Yes… quite! In-Betweens are connections through time and space. Places where those who know how can travel to and fro."

"Those who know?"

George and Aunt Lexi answered in unison, "Yes!"

"Carry on with your studies," said Lexi. "Have you reached the Age of Dragon?"

Ava buried her nose deep within the book. She found the Age of Dragon and read through it, trying not to worry, because some of the things that happened, and that were forecast to happen, were frightening. It was hard to explain, but she felt that there was more not said than said. It was neither as warm as previous Ages, nor as enlightened. She grew restless.

"What's wrong Ava?"

"I don't like this Age of Dragon. Something about it makes me very nervous. My energy feels drained just reading it. Does that make sense?"

"Perfectly! This is not surprising, Ava, because it is your opposite. It is fire while you are water. It is also the age where we see the most frightening beings born, and I don't just mean dragons."

"Yes, I read about some of them, like salamanders and the Banshee. Let me see..."

> *A banshee is a death spirit who is heard to wail with screams when someone is about to die. She is said to have fiery red eyes from her weeping but no one who has seen her has lived to tell the tale.*

Turning the page Ava read on while all in the car were silent. Tarran in particular was enthralled.

> *It is worth noting further that the Age of Dragon also saw the rise of the Djinn or Genie in our world. The Djinn can manifest any wishes a mortal desires but always at a cost. Genies are first and foremost tricksters, thus the need to keep these mischievous elementals at a distance.*

Ava sat back.

"I've heard the Banshee's wail," she said.

Silence in the car. And fear.

"That's the sound I tried to describe to Aunt Winifred the morning I collapsed in the forest."

"But you are still alive," said Tarran.

"Thankfully. Maybe it's only people from Ireland who are touched by the cry? And what about Robin Goodfellow? Isn't he a Djinn?"

"It's true that he is a trickster with a wicked streak," said George, "but a Djinn? They are the agents of darkness. They hate human beings with such passion that they will think nothing of destroying this world."

"I doubt that Robin Goodfellow thinks much of anything except himself," Ava decided.

"He served King Oster and Queen Amber," said Tarran. "The Djinn hate everything, not just humans but also Fae. How could one infiltrate so deeply into the Royal household? It makes no sense."

"It does make sense if you think about it," said George. "The age they were born was an age of fire, and the last royal household before that was Selkie, the Age of Water. They are elemental opposites so Robin would have had time to work his way into both. Consider the power he and his like have gained if this is true. It would mean they have been the enemy within for aeons. They are pure evil manifest as energy into an entity of hatred, deceit, envy and greed and they can operate in many guises, many forms. They will do anything in their power to destroy humans, Fae and all our worlds. And I'm not sure whether we have the power to stop them."

George slumped back into the seat. Tarran and Lexi were pale. Ava was trying to take it all in, but she was more excited than scared.

Meanwhile, oblivious to it all, the twenty-first century car sped on smoothly through the English countryside.

19. Morgan

The car finally reached Berwick upon Tweed and Lexi followed the signs to the harbour. There, a wonderful site befell them, for Aunt Ellie Windrush was waiting. Her bright orange and yellow African dress stood out against the backdrop of green sea and blue sky. She reminded Ava of an Earth Goddess, as if power shone from her. The minute she saw Ava she held out her arms and said, "Come, beautiful girl, let me embrace you."

Aunt Ellie's hugs were the best in the world. She wrapped you in her arms and love and warmth flowed through you.

"Morgan?" Ava asked, rather cautiously.

"Humpf! That boy! No doubt his personal taxi will bring him."

On cue, a police car veered around the corner, stopping in front of Aunt Ellie. Two policemen got out and tipped their hats to her. One approached, the other opened the passenger door.

Out stepped Morgan.

"Thank you so much, Officer Johnston, always a pleasure."

Aunt Ellie sighed, "This time?"

"Trying to steal the contents of the gumball machine at the arcades, Miss Ellie."

Ellie Windrush looked as if she was about to explode, then said, "Morgan, boy, you are going to end up in a bad place. I've told you before and I tell you again."

"Indeed ma'am, that's precisely what we've been saying. We have given him another warning, but if he continues on this path, well, you know. And he knows, too."

"Yes, officer, thank you. Come here, Morgan, and say hello to Ava and Tarran. Take a leaf out of their books."

Morgan raised his eyebrow in disgust.

Elizabeth Windrush had married a Scottish fisherman from Aberdeen, but when Morgan was only three years old, his father had been killed at sea leaving Elizabeth to raise him - one of those thirteen mysterious deaths. Morgan occasionally went off the rails... weekly, it seemed. His behaviour resulted in him being expelled from every school in Aberdeenshire, including the surrounding counties. Now, no-one wanted him anywhere near any educational establishment.

Yet despite his bad boy persona, Ava liked Morgan. He had a sweet nature hidden beneath a rebellious streak. He also had beautiful big blue-green eyes and a blond afro. Although not as tall as Tarran he was taller than Ava. And of course, he was forever in trouble. He gave Lexi and Ava a hug, but greeted Tarran only by name which received an equal response of 'Morgan.'

When George stepped out of the car, Morgan saw his colourful garb and was about to laugh when Ava elbowed him in the ribs.

"Commander Wrenn," said Ellie, "it is good to see you again."

"You too Ellie but how did you know to meet us here?"

"Brenna and Fawn on their way up to Jissika stopped off to tell us what had been happening. We'd been making our way down to the manor when Holly sent us a message."

"Email?"

"Crow."

Tarran sniffed and might have said something he'd regret, but George's shadow re-appeared and whispered something in his owner's ear.

"Are you sure?" George said. "Good work! See what else you can discover. Robin Goodfellow, bah!"

Ava whispered to Morgan, "Hateful being. We've had two encounters with him already. George seems to dislike him more than most, though."

"Robin was George's second in command at the Battle of Poppies," said Morgan, "thousands of years ago. It was one of the greatest battles in Fae history. Poppies were originally white you know but after the battle so many had lost their lives, that the ground was stained red with blood, so poppies now are red."

"Rubbish!" said Tarran.

"Oh, right, Sir Tarran. Is it my fault your hoity-toity education doesn't teach you that?"

"At least I have an education."

"Being thrown out of every school is a lifestyle choice, Sir Posh."

"Stop it the pair of you," Ava ordered.

Tarran folded his arms and turned away from Morgan but winked at Ava.

"Shall we attend to our quest and lay aside your adolescent arguments for the moment?" George asked. "The army of Lost Souls are on the Holy Island."

"The army of the Damned?" Morgan asked, excited.

He was always looking for trouble, if trouble didn't come looking for him. And a battle with the army of Lost Souls souls was right up his street. Ellie shook her head in despair.

"Come on," said George, "if we want to make the tide, let's head for the Lindisfarne ferry now. I don't know what we are going to find there, but we need to go. Now."

"We're going to need your special talents, Ellie," said Lexi. "I know it."

Lindisfarne stood alone and mysterious on a piece of land rising up from the sea. A solitary mound of earth surrounded by water with an abbey on the summit. Morgan surveyed the area eagerly wanting to see the Army of the Damned, but no such luck. As they disembarked at Holy Island Harbour, they were told the last ferry back to mainland was at 5pm and not to be late.

"No need to worry about the return journey," said Morgan. "We must stay till dark."

"Why?" Ava asked.

"Because that's when the fun starts. Aye? Stick with me and I'll keep you safe. You can trust me with your life."

"Thank you Morgan, but I can look after myself."

They decided to scout around, especially the area close to Queen Elizabeth's building works. They would keep fairly close together, prepared for unexpected and unwelcome visitors. The land allowed this for though barren, it was not easy to get lost.

The group made their way to the castle. Standing on the

battlements they each ventured to a corner, although Ava had Tarran on one side and Morgan on the other. Each of them sending dagger looks to the other. Ava shook her head and opened her mouth to tell them both off when a loudspeaker announcement interrupted.

"Could all visitors requiring the ferry back to the mainland please make their way to the ferry terminal. We have a severe storm warning and the castle and abbey will be closing in half an hour. Thank you."

"Coincidence?" Ava asked Ellie.

"I think not. Come, take my hand, everyone, in a circle. Here hold my hand, Ava. Let's call upon some African wonder. Repeat after me…"

And they intoned the following charm:

> *siri katika macho.*
> Siri katika macho.
> *Kufanya hivyo usiku.*
> Kufanya hivyo usiku.
> *Siri katika macho Kufanya hivyo usiku.*
> Siri katika macho Kufanya hivyo usiku.

"What are we saying?" Ava whispered to Morgan.

"Unseen in sight, make it night."

Holding hands tightly, time sped round, but no one saw them. To others, they were invisible, encased in spells. The world was spinning one way and they another. They were widdershins while the world went deosil, floating above the battlements.

Ava saw the storm coming across the sea, darker clouds chasing a thick, ominous darkness.

They spun closer to the battlement until they touched down and stopped. Quiet, not a sound. It was no longer day.

"If what we seek is here, we need to find it before that army," said Ellie pointing to the approaching darkness. "It is the Army of the Damned."

Tarran and Morgan strained their necks searching the water to see what appeared to be a giant wave approaching.

"Force field," George ordered, as if they all would know what he meant. "Except you three. There's little time, go find the horn."

"How?"

"Use your instincts Ava. Remember the power is within you," and George joined Ellie and Lexi on each corner of the battlements.

A feeling of such power welled up inside Ava. The words formed in her heart and seeing them in her mind, she shouted them out.

> *Show me what others cannot see.*
> *Show me the Horn of Bran so that I may free*
> *all those that mean so much to me.*

On the final word, a huge crack echoed round as a lightning bolt shot from the sky. A piece of the battlement exploded and illuminated a staircase as axes, swords and arrows hit the force field encasing the castle.

"Tarran," Ellie urged him, "we need you. We are stronger as four. You are a son of The Thirteen, take the left flank."

"But…"

"Morgan, go with Ava and bring the horn. Do you hear me?"

"Yes, ma, I hear you."

Ava didn't wait for Morgan to act. She virtually pulled him down the narrow spiral staircase. Reluctantly, Tarran joined the three adult and reached out to strengthen the force field as lightning sparked round them, ferocious and fearsome.

Through the flashes, the illuminated haunted faces of the damned could be seen clearly. They still wore their Viking helmets, despite eternal damnation. They were the north men who had crushed the Saints under foot at Lindisfarne. They were brave and victorious, and they were damned and they were here.

The force field broke as the damned rained down upon them in an endless torrent. George grabbed Tarran, trying to create a second barrier for the staircase, but before they could complete it, a huge black crow with iridescent purple feathers flew straight at them.

George tried to grab at it screaming, "Goodfellow!" as Tarran called after Morgan and Ava.

"I don't know if you can hear me, but whatever you're doing, do it fast. Do you hear me Morgan? Ava? Get out of there? Now!"

But it was too late. Another bolt of lightning sent the remains of the battlements crashing down the staircase, covering the opening.

Ava and Morgan were on their own with Robin Goodfellow.

20. The Battle

The staircase seemed to go on forever, deep into the depths of the Earth. The castle had built its dungeons as close to hell as possible. Extinguished torches lined the walls and Morgan lit each one as they passed by. The stairs themselves had started wide but narrowed, making it dangerous to run. At the bottom, the space was tiny. On either side were two closed doors formed from bars of gold.

They pulled and pushed each one, but neither opened. Grabbing one of the torches, Ava could see something glinting silver in the fire light through the bars of the door on the left.

"Morgan, it's the horn, I'm sure it is."

Morgan peered through the flickering darkness.

"Yes, it could be."

Ava pulled at the door but it remained locked.

A familiar screech echoed down the staircase.

"Morgan, he's found us! Robin Goodfellow."

"Hold the torch, Ava. We're not leaving empty handed."

He reached into his pocket and came out with a hair grip. Ava watched as Morgan used his somewhat dubious lock picking skills to wrest open the dungeon door.

And he did.

Above them, the battle raged as lightning flashed and thunder roared around the castle. Every so often they would hear the clattering of swords and what sounded like yelling and shouting but that did not drown out the harrowing screech as Robin Goodfellow flew down the dungeon steps.

Ava shone the torch upwards into the intermittent darkness of the staircase and saw a huge dark mass swirling towards them.

Just as door clicked.

"Finally!" and Morgan disappeared into the blackness.

Ava turned back to the staircase to confront the huge mass which was almost upon her. As it descended, it changed shape.

First legs, then body, arms, neck and head.

Robin Goodfellow.

He stepped from mid-air onto the ground.

"At last, little one, all alone are we? Abandoned by family and friends? Your father was a fool to write what he did. I punished him, and your mother will be next. But you, alone and weak, what shall I do to you? Torture? Imprison? Charm? Kill?"

Out of the darkness brandishing the Horn of Bran, Morgan shouted, "You and whose army?" and without fear or hesitation he plunged the horn into Robin Goodfellow's neck.

An excruciating scream echoed round the confined space. Ava covered her ears but Morgan grabbed her hand pulled her towards the other door.

"Time to leave," he said. With the Horn in one hand and Ava holding the other, Morgan took one almighty kick at the barred door and it fell to the floor.

"Just like school gates. Come on, don't look back, hurry."

As she ran up the staircase, Ava glimpsed Robin Goodfellow oozing purple blood from his neck. Flowing from the open wound, it turned to smoke, covering him until he dissolved with screams of agony.

They raced through the room and up the other staircase which led them to a completely different part of Lindisfarne, near the cliffs and nowhere near the battlements.

The army of the Lost Souls sensed the change in command and turned their gaze towards Ava and Morgan. The roar of the sea silenced Morgan's shouts. Lightning flashed, illuminating the scene of jagged cliffs and white waves crashing down upon the rocks.

"We have to climb over the railing, it's the only way," he called as best he could above the deafening sounds.

"I can't!" Ava said, fearing the terrible drop.

"We have to get away from them. They are gaining on us. The cliff is our only chance."

A crash of thunder shook the railing. Morgan reached out to to pull her over but she couldn't move. There was only one way he could get her to climb over.

"I dare you!" he challenged her, as they'd challenged each

other many times over many years, but never like this.

Ava bit her lip and grabbed the rail. An icy spray of crashing waves upon the cliff made Morgan turn to see a huge wall of water racing towards them. He grabbed hold of the rail. Ava saw what was coming and entwined her arms around the rail, she on one side, Morgan on the other. They closed their eyes, crouching close to the safety rail, praying it would hold them both.

Sheet lightning flashed as the giant wave crashed over them. Ava could feel her legs sweep up as if she was flying, and the icy water lashed and punched her with all its force. She held onto the safety rail tighter, banging her chin on it as the wave pushed her down further. All she could hear was the overwhelming sound of rushing water. Her eyes firmly shut, she didn't know what was happening to Morgan.

Why had they come here?

Why did she have to be the one?

She wasn't a part of this world anyway.

All she could feel was the rail and the sea lifting her and turning her. Freezing hands pulled her away from the railing. She held her breath but needed to breathe. Her body dropped to the ground and as she gasped the cool, salty air, she heard someone calling her name.

She opened her eyes. Lightning still flashed round them and waves still crashed into the cliffs below, but now she was on the other side and Morgan was behind the rail. Leaping over and grabbing her hand, he pulled her closer to the cliffs.

"Did you feel them?"

"Who?"

"Them! Pulling you? They want us to go with them. They are here to help us."

"No, Morgan, they cannot be trusted, everyone has told us so."

"Would you rather face - that?"

Behind, she saw the army of souls racing towards her and Morgan, their swords pointing meancingly, only the deafening thunder and crashing waves silenced their shouts of hatred and revenge.

"What should we do?"

"When the next wave comes, let the sea take you. They are in the waves."

Pulling Ava closer to the edge, Morgan saw a giant wave, racing towards them. Would it get to them in time? The army had now reached the rail. Morgan squeezed Ava's hand. They had no choice.

"Do you trust me?"

Ava hesitated, then remembering what Morgan had said to her earlier that day, "Yes, with my life."

"Then *jump*!"

Morgan leapt into the air, still holding tightly to Ava, their hands entwined. Ava could no longer feel the ground. They had leapt from the cliff.

I fall, I die, I am no more.
I am flying once more...

21. Callanish III

A seagull's cry and the fresh salty breeze coaxed Ava to open her eyes. In front of her was a sight to behold. On a rocky beach, hundreds of little heads bobbed up and down in the water. Gazing as far out as she could, Ava watched the beautiful mermaid heads of rainbow colours. Occasionally, a tail would flip as one dived into her watery home. Morgan lay unconscious beside her, still holding the horn.

"He's alright," said a sweet voice, "he is protected by the horn."

Before her, in a deep pool, was the same beautiful face she had seen at the royal court in Fae - the tall lady who had said she would see Ava again. She was half in the water but the occasional lap of a wave exposed the beauty of her tail. All the blues and greens of the sea shimmered on her scales. Her long blond hair fell below her waist and the front was tied off her exquisite face by a tiara made of pearls and corals.

"My name is Mariella and I have been waiting for you for a long time Ava. We were all so relieved when you said yes to the King's request."

"All?"

"My sisters and brothers," and she waved her hand to the mer people bobbing up and down behind her. They waved back and swam closer to Ava, each with a different coloured tail.

"We are the same but different. We are all individual but one. Just as the Fae whose wings are coloured by the age they are born in, so too are our fins. Some of us have red because we were born in the Age of Dragon, some have yellow for the Age of Griffin, some green for the Age of Unicorn."

Ava strained to see Mariella's tail.

"Mine is blue. I am born in the same age as you, the Age of Selkie. We are both of water, emotion and time, forever flowing, ever running."

Morgan stirred and woke, staring at the vision before him.

"Welcome back," said Ava.

Morgan had no time to speak.

"We need to move quickly if you are to return to your aunts," said Mariella. "It is Midsummer morning after all and the horn must be returned to the Castle of Glass."

"Can you take me to the castle? My father is there. I could…"

"I can't, but I can take you somewhere better. However, I must travel by foot," and with that Mariella inched herself out of the pool. She held on to the rock and as soon as the air reached her tail it started to change shape, morphing wonderfully into legs. She climbed out of the water in a glistening array of gold, turquoise and cyan clothes. Looking at them close up, Ava realised these were not human clothes at all but Fae garments, soft, enchanted material made from scales and coral and other sea life. Ava touched the silk skirt which was the softest she'd ever felt, like liquid in the palm of her hand.

"Sea silk," said Mariella, "your ancient Romans called it Byssus, it is joined with sea weed thread."

"It's beautiful, Mariella."

"You may have one too, one day. We are both daughters of water remember?"

Both Ava and Morgan realised that the mer people had not just saved them, they had carried them to a different island. This was no longer Lindisfarne. Above them was the standing stone of Callanish.

"Where are we?" Ava asked.

"The Isle of Lewis. We brought you on the orders of Jissika Ataksak. Look, she conjures."

Hidden behind the stones Ava could see the sky changing beautiful colours of reds, pinks, yellows; the fire of sunrise was beginning. Midsummer morning was upon them. She closed her eyes and could hear the Inuit chant of her aunt.

"Come, we must be quick for the hour is passing."

Mariella rushed forward. Her sprint could have been swimming on land, so graceful and fluid. Morgan couldn't take his eyes off her. Nor could Ava.

As they approached the stones, they heard other voices in the chant, yet only her aunt was present. The song was melodic and enchanting. Aunt Jissika sang with an indescribably beauty and mystery, her arms raised towards the sky, her eyes closed.

"They are the voices of the thirteen who have gone before," and she gestured toward the thirteen stones. "Rise now sisters and join me once again."

Of the thirteen stones, only eight were standing; five fallen ones lay strewn about the ground.

Mariella glided over to Jissika, bringing the two young people.

"Come now Ava, we must send you home. You too Morgan, hold on to that horn. We have not much time," and Aunt Jissika joined in with the chant once more. "Stand in the centre. We will do the rest."

They did as they were told.

"I've been here before," said Ava, "many years ago. I know this place. This is Callanish III. Thirteen stones."

"Thirteen Gatekeepers, my girl. The original Thirteen. Rise now sisters," Aunt Jissika commanded.

The fallen stones started to move as the sky above formed a mass of swirling cloud.

"Hold on to me Ava, remember what I said. I'll never let you go."

"Trust me, Morgan, I won't let you go," said Ava, only half believing what she was seeing.

The silver base of the horn glinted in the Midsummer sunrise. The Inuit chanting gathered around them as the stones creaked to life and stood, taking their rightful place next to their sisters. The cloud above them swirled and grew with each passing rotation until at last it covered the entire area.

Mariella and Aunt Jissika carried on chanting. The deep haunting voice of Jissika rose above the others as Ava and Morgan defied gravity and hovered above ground.

"They know what they are doing. At least, I hope they do," said Morgan looking down.

Ava closed her eyes. She sensed they were flying and held on tightly to Morgan as he held on to her. The swirling sound of air and clouds brushing past her drowned out the chant of Aunt Jissika and The Thirteen. All she could hear now was the whistling wind and rushing air. It was all she could do not to scream. They swirled, twisting round together in the tornado of Midsummer mystery. Floating and swirling, a dance of time and enchantment. They dared look. Colours of life, ribbons of dreams flowed around them, cascading into an eternal river that ran throughout the universe.

They allowed this to sweep them along until, in the distance, they could sense a different chant, one that both of them had heard before.

22. Midsummer

The sound grew clearer and louder as they swirled and twisted through the air until the familiar, gentle voice of Winifred rose higher than the others. Ava opened her eyes to see the Heart of the Forest beneath them.

The swirling slowed and the dizzying colours faded. They descended to the centre of the stone circle where every seat of The Thirteen was taken. George took Aunt Jessika's place, Morgan and Ava, grateful to be on Terra Firma again, waited to see where they should go. Tarran joined them.

"You'll never guess! We sailed here!"

"We just flew," siad Morgan, unimpressed.

Not to be outdone Tarran replied, "The car changed into a submarine and we travelled faster than the speed of light."

"We travelled in the heart of a tornado."

"We saw mermaids."

"Mermaids saved us."

Someon had to stop the rivalry.

"Gentlemen," said George, "and ladies, if you please. Heads up. Incoming."

Tarran, Morgan and Ava all raised their heads. A black mass was heading towards them.

"The Army of the Damned?"

"No. The Nothingness. The Entity itself."

"Quickly Morgan," George ordered, "place the Horn of Bran on the altar. Ava, I need you to do your thing again." Ava looked baffled. "Ava who stopped time?" George said, "who opened the room that was barred to all else? Who unlocked the Book of Shadows? Who gave form to a lost father? These things don't happen for no reason. They happen for the person you are. This force comes from within you. Who has just travelled through an ancient gate closed for three millennia? You, my child. We need you to believe once more or this quest will be over before its begun."

"I can't. I don't know how."

"Dream it, feel it, see it, believe it."

The Thirteen chanted

> *Dream it, feel it, see it, believe it.*
> *Dream it, feel it, see it, believe it.*

Ava stared at the horn on the altar. She closed her eyes. She could hear her aunts' voices chanting. She repeated the words in her mind, "*Dream it, feel it, see it, believe it.*"

The horn's image was emblazoned on her mind like the brightest light stared at for too long. She imagined the ancient Book of Shadows standing alone in its pride of place. She could see the horn on top of the book.

'I am dreaming this. I am feeling this. I am seeing this. I believe this.'

Her aunts still chanted as the black mass morphed and shifted. When Ava opened her eyes, the horn had gone.

"Well done, Ava. Come stand next to me. Let's banish this evil."

Ava ran to her aunt and glancing round the circle saw all her aunts there except Jissika. George had taken her place for now. Tarran stood next to his mother and Morgan stood next to Ellie who winked at Ava.

In the sky, the black mass had grown giant wings, slowly flapping, holding the huge Entity together.

> *Black night. White knight.*
> *Banish this evil from my sight.*

The Thirteen repeated the spell over and over again.

> *Black night. White knight.*
> *Banish this evil from my sight.*

The words echoed around the Heart of the Forest. The sky darkened and seemed to shake. The black mass started to change shape and, astonishingly, to break apart. Creatures, something like birds but ugly and venomous, separated from the roiling mass. They squawked and cackled their hideous cries as they dive bombed the stone circle. And still the spell was cast. The women stood, unafraid, chanting their spell.

Out of the clouds emerged a massive swarm of crows led by a black swan. They shrieked and dived and sent the flying creatures tumbling and squawking into countless different directions. The crows never let up, chasing them until not one was left and the heart of the Entity vanished in mist of black despair.

The swan descended, the most elegant, glossy, beautiful, massive black bird Ava could ever hope to see. It bowed to her and to George and to Winifred who reciprocated.

"The Swan of St. Hugh," whispered Tarran.

"All things connect," said George.

The swan then took one giant leap into the air, flapping its enormous wings in an almost vertical take-off, and sailed away, watched by the grateful onlookers on the ground.

Silence. Relief. Joy.

Shattered by Lexi clapping her hands and shouting, 'Happy Midsummer!' before bursting into laughter, at which point the other aunts joined in, cheering and shaking hands. Even Tarran and Morgan gave each other a friendly pat on the back, though Morgan's pat nearly put Tarran into the stone table, which sent George into hysterics.

"Happy Midsummer, all my wonderful aunts," said Ava.

23. Secrets

The Midsummer celebration went on all day and night. There was food, dancing and singing, even the royal court made an appearance. George changed back into the little blue-winged being to greet their Majesties. All manner of fae appeared, dressed in their finest Midsummer attire, including fauns, satyresses, pixies, brownies, gnomes, hobgoblins, oracles and elves.

Morgan, Tarran and Ava sat watching the fauns dance with the dryads and nymphs.

"Who'd have thought? Just look at this!"

"Aye, and with just one of the treasures. Can you imagine what the party will be like when we have all thirteen?"

"Mmm! I don't even want to think about it. Be back soon," she said hurriedly, leaving Tarran and Morgan to the attentions of two wood nymphs.

She found Aunt Winifred in the libraray.

"Aunt?"

Winifred was placing the horn in a decorative box encased by beams of light. She waved her hand in a cross shape and sealed it with a softly intoned spell.

"No-one's getting that then?"

"Hello, my darling Ava. Not until its needed, no."

Ava gently swept her hand over the Book of Shadows, tracing the outline of the embossed leather. The room was quiet despite the celebrations going on outside. Aunt Winifred quietly spoke.

"I suppose you want to know about your mother?"

Ava could not speak, but she said yes with her eyes.

Aunt Winifred took a deep breath.

"Sweeheart, you'll never believe it…"

The Codex : A Reference

The Hieroglyphic Fae
The Sacred Language of Fairies

by
Professor R. G. Fellow

Edited by
Flora-Beth Edwards

Dedicated to Ava...
Do not follow me on this path...

Contents

A Little Introduction

The language of faeries is derived from nature. In the British Isles, home of the Fae there are many influences. The language of the Fae has grown alongside its counterpart and just as human society was influenced by different peoples, so too has the fairy language.

We all know about Hieroglyphs; the writing of ancient Egypt. They are quite fascinating to look at due to their recognisable pictures of people, animals, plants and all manner of images from nature.

As Monsieur Jean-Francois Champollion began to decipher the strange pictures on ancient Egyptian walls and monuments, he had little idea of the great impact he would have. He was in fact, creating a new language which would become one of the most famous languages in the world.

These delightful pictures are placed together in rows and columns to form endless patterns of words. These wonderful words are not just pretty pictures on walls they tell a story and they are a written record of a people gone but never forgotten. The amazing monuments of Egypt such as the pyramids, sphinx, and tombs remind us daily of a fascinating society.

The language of faeries from the British Isles is very similar. The wee folk have left their mark upon this land and inevitably the world for wherever there is a descendent of the British Isles, the enchanted realm goes with them.

The first part of this book gives short explanations of the history of Faery language and writing systems. It examines the decipherment of Faeroglyphs after the ability to read them had been lost due to various episodes of human interference.

The workings of Faeroglyphs are covered next with explanations of their different functions such as the direction of writing and how Faeroglyphs are written out in English or transliteration.

Then we look at the most common Faeroglyphs you may have seen and have been unaware of their meaning. Further, we shall how to discover how to write your own name in Fae.

Then we shall delve a little further into grammar, and look at plurals, numbers, gender and verbs.

The second part of the book uncovers the history of the enchanted realm and most notably, Faeriec words and names in Faeroglyphs which give descriptions of what Fairies think about times, seasons, life after death, gods and goddesses, and what being a fairy today is truly like.

Few humans return from the enchanted realm to their world without wanting to know more about the Fae. However, now with this book you can begin to discover their ancient language and ask these delightful little beings to come back into the human world. But be warned! Fairies can be tricksters and you may just end up in their world unable to get back!

Further, if you do decide to go hunting for fairies, do take with you a notebook to be used as your field study book. A good Faeologist always has a note book with them to be used for drawing and record keeping of encounters with the Fey.

Good luck!

Terminology

There are many spellings of the enchanted realm with the common word being; Fairy.

However, there are also other terms such as Fay, Fae, Faery, and Faerie.

Therefore, within this book the word Fae refers to the language of fairies. Here is a list of words concerning Fairies:

- Fae =Language – Academic usage of the beings of Fay
- Fairies = Generic spelling of the people,
- Similar usage, the people of Britain are called British.
- Faeries = Respectful spelling of the beings from Fay.
- Fay = The land the Fey come from.
- Faeriec = Objects, places, and people within the realm of Fae.
- Fey, Fae = People of Fay.

NB: It is worth pointing out to the untrained that this indeed can be all highly confusing. The terminology itself is only used in such high observance when meeting royalty within Fay, and never when working alongside the common Fey themselves.

A Little History

Oldest Writing System

Human beings have always drawn and we have always communicated with each other in some form. In every part of the world pictures on caves, rocks, even deserts have been found.

Our ancestors have been communicating with us since the beginning of time. As we look around the world at the pictures and images left behind we can still hear their voices.

The same is true of Fairies.

Spoken Language

Only one language was written in Faeroglyphs and that was the language of fairies; the Fae of the British Isles. Unlike its human counterpart, the language of the Fae has not changed. The English language of Shakespeare and Chaucer are both very different of what is spoken and written today.

That is the beauty of language, it is alive. Language twists and turns with each new generation whose youth and vibrancy bring something different to it.

The language of fairies is derived from nature. In the British Isles, home of the Fae, there are many influences. The language of the Fae has grown alongside its human counterpart and just as human society was as influenced by different invading peoples, so too has the fairy language.

When we begin to look at Faeroglyphs you will see images from all manner of things and you will recognise them from different cultures. The Omega symbol of ancient Greece Ω can be found in the language of fairies as can the Beith or Beth from ancient Ireland;

These two symbols show the diversity of the Fae as one stems from ancient Greece whilst the other forms part of the

Beíth/
Beth

human Celtic Ogham Alphabet.

The Celtic Tree Ogham or Ogam, is one of the Ogham alphabets used across Ireland, Scotland, Wales, and the Isle of Man, and dates back to the 5th Century and is believed to have been used by our Celtic ancestors for divination. (Figure 1)

The alphabet consists of twenty letters each corresponding

to a tree which carries with it divinatory meanings. For the pedantic amongst humans, although it is called the Celtic Tree Ogham, it not only has trees but also other plants and shrubbery.

The Beith, or Beth is the letter B and means beginnings, initiations, cleansing and birth. The tree it represents is the Birch tree, the first tree to leaf in spring and also the first tree which colonises cleared land.

This knowledge of nature, in particular, trees and plants, the fairies understand and knew as this is their home; the world of nature. The other trees used in the Fae:

S = Willow/Saille,
H = Hawthorne/Huath
D = Oak/Duir
Q = Apple/Quert
M = Bramble/Muin
U = Heather/Ur

The rest of their alphabet is made of symbols and images derived from fairies' interactions in their everyday world.

Figure 1

Ogham Alphabet

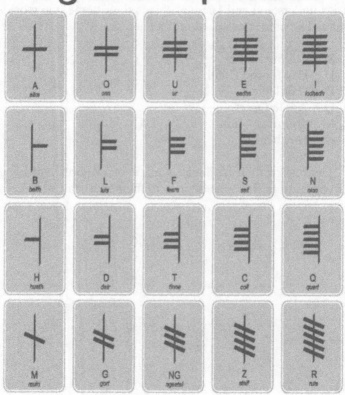

The Fae have always been here and much longer than humans. Human beings are the new addition in this world and our history is a direct response to their presence.

The stories of Snow White, Sleeping Beauty, and Cinderella to name but a few are stories the human world has grown up with. The Fae crept into our sleeping dreams of night and took hold within our unconsciousness.

Mystical, magical beings who can guide, play, come to our rescue or damn us have been with us since the beginning. Yet the true nature of their world, their language, and their histories still remain lost to us.

The Fae only allow us to see just a part of their world. The history of the Fae is mixed with humans. The beginning histories believed that fairies were fallen angels or the souls of unbaptised children. While others have unfairly regarded the Fae as the heathen dead and therefore neither good enough for Heaven nor bad enough for Hell.

Yet nothing could be further from the truth. The last two examples of explanations for faeries are obviously from the Christian era but as we know, faeries pre-date Christianity.

However, it was only in the Christian era that we began to write these as originally, they had been legends. These stories had passed along the generations as part of the oral story telling round camp fires of communities.

Every culture in every part of the world has some form of fairy or elemental being. What they truly are or what their real purpose is, only a chosen few mortals ever really know.

Faeries are beings of nature; they are elementals of air, fire, earth, and water. Their language and the subsequent Faeroglyphs which developed are representations of their history and their way of life.

The written language of Fae was slower to develop than the spoken language. Faeroglyphs were a kind of formal writing similar to our writing on monuments, detailing a famous person or battle. The old illuminated medieval manuscripts are also similar in many ways to the development of Fae.

However, it became ever more apparent to the Fae that their world was under threat from human interference. So, it was decided by Faery Monarchs in the third dynasty to leave a lasting record of their presence. Remember, the fairies' world is one of nature, the earth, and every forest, ocean, jungle, desert, woodland, and stream is their home.

The human presence would dictate the faeries history and subsequently their language.

What Are Faeroglyphs?

Faeroglyphs are similar to their ancient Egyptian counterpart Hieroglyphs. Both these forms of writing incorporate images and pictures from nature and the world in general.

In the beginning, Champollion thought there were 864 different signs. However, with the advent of further study and excavation it has been found there were several thousand at various times in human history. Unfortunately, nothing like this exists in Faeriec lore.

The Fae language in the British Isles is very similar to our alphabet with 26 letters and all the words fairies use are made up of these.

The word Faeroglyphs is a noun. A noun is the name of a person, place, thing, or idea. While Faeroglyphic is, an adjective and should not be used as a noun. An adjective is a describing word. Adjectives are usually placed just before the words they qualify such as tiny fairy, or, three fairy horses.

Adjectives are words that makes a noun more specific such as stinky fairy. Therefore, the correct usage is: Faeroglyphs and Faeroglyphic signs.

Also found in the language, or Fae, are the use of pictograms. We find pictogram usage in the number section of this book.

Pictograms are pictures of objects and through its pictorial resemblance of a real object. The very early written symbols of human beings were pictograms as they were pictures which resemble what they signify such as a boat, or a bear on a cave wall.

They can be found in every part of the world and used even today in parts of Africa, Americas, and the Oceanic regions.

Further, today we see them all over in use as road signs, or health and safety signs. Such as No Entry, or Pedestrian Crossing:

Further, Faeriec and human society are still influencing each other with the human fascination of crop circles. These are amazing pictograms that appear in fields during the night. Are the Fae still trying to tell us something? Most of the crop circles are images of different things from DNA strands to geometric shapes. Whilst some still consist of very large and intricate rings and lines.

These circles and pictograms are formed in crops such as wheat and rye which are flattened either by the wind or Fairies? But no human has ever discovered a fairy creating them...yet!

Figure 2 Crop Circle Pictogram Designs

The Fairy Scribe

When it was realised by the Faeriec population that something must be done to preserve the Fae history and language, special assemblies were set up to devise a form of recording and recognising the past, present, and future.

The first Faeroglyphic counsel was set up in the Age of Unicorn, in human years some 250,000 years ago.

A number of rather young Faeries from certain distinguished households were chosen to become scribes. It is not known how many of the Faeriec population could actually read and write from that time but we do know, that now fairy schools are very common and at least one member of a household must attend school. They in turn pass the knowledge to the rest of the fairy house.

However, in the beginning to be chosen to become a scribe was a very privileged and prestigious act. Those fairies that did become scribes were treated with such respect as they almost became royal.

Indeed, many scribes often did enter into royal households and become monarchs themselves such was the respect placed upon those who could read and write.

The training for Fae scribes or Writshtars as they are known in Fae was a rather long task. Writshtars went to school for three yanni.

To understand the length of time spent at school, one yanni is equivalent to one hundred earth years. Therefore, Writshtars went to school for three hundred years. Though what we know of the lifespan of the average fairy this isn't very long really. When an average healthy fairy can live for at least ten thousand years; three hundred years at school is nothing.

Faeroglyphs were mainly carved in rocks and stones that is why we find many stones with strange markings on as this is how Writshtars began to write by carving lines and shapes. They then progressed onto figures and on a much larger scale which can still be seen today, such as, the White Horse of Uffington, or giant of Cerne Abbis. These giant pictograms can be seen the world over including Peru with the Nazca lines, and once again, the giants in the desert. (Figure 3)

Nazca Giants and Lines : Figure 3

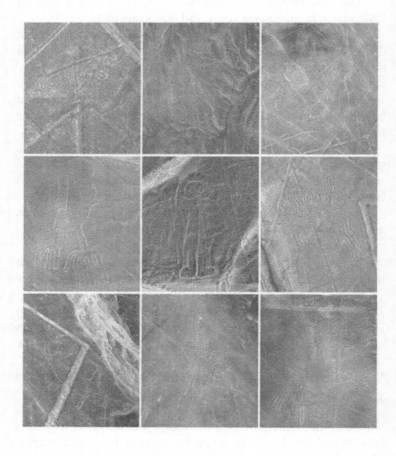

However, here in the British Isles the Fae always worked within nature and for nature. The favourite pictogram they would use was the horse that is why we have so many horses carved into hillsides.

However, we also have the Vale of the Red Horse. The Red Horse of Tysoe was cut once again into the earth but instead of white chalk, the land of South Warwickshire has red clay and the horse became red.

Unfortunately, humans planted trees over the hose in the last century and the Red Horse will never be seen again.

The Faeroglyphic language we see today is a result of training through the millenniums. Faeriec works were written on thin rolls of bark from silver birch trees which grew abundantly throughout the land. The white peeling bark was allowed to naturally to fall from the tree before it could be used and then refined and filed down even further for the Fae to write upon.

The silver birch is a highly-respected tree in Fay for not only is its bark used by faeries for writing on but it is a tree which has so much magic surrounding it. Its other name is Warty Birch, and its leaves are slightly triangular which turn yellow in autumn. The flowers are catkins which faeries adore flying on and in spring forms a part of the Catkins Derby.

Further, many species of birds, animals and insects including butterflies and moths are all used extensively by the Fae as methods of transportation.

Moreover, the silver birch has an open canopy which allows light to reach the ground enabling many plants, mosses, and grasses to grow safely around it. The majority of these plants form the central base of Faeriec kingdoms. Flowering plants found in birch woods include primrose, violets, bluebells, wood anemone, and also wood sorrel, not to mention cowberry.

Furthermore, the branches have tangled masses of twigs growing among them known locally as witch's brooms. The silver birch is undoubtedly one of the most important trees in Fay.

The peeling silver bark is also highly regarded just as precious as any gold or jewels of the human world. As silver birch bark is the material that the Royal Fae crowns of the West are made from.

Pens and Ink

The pens used by the Writshtars was daisy stalks. The first daisy of spring was regarded as the perfect pen and was highly prized with student Writshtars paying out huge sums for one. If the Writshtar could not get their hands on a daisy stalk then an ivy stalk was the next best thing and was far cheaper due to it being very common.

The favourite colour among faeries was and is a rainbow. In human society, a rainbow is an arch with seven colours in it; red, orange, yellow, green, blue, indigo and violet. The way we humans remember the sequence is: Richard of York gave battle in vain. Thus, even the ways humans remember the spectrum of colours of a rainbow was by the events of a battle.

However, for faeries, rainbow is a colour. The stalks were magically taken to each plant of colour so that it took on that colour until the stalk is full of rainbow. The Writshtar would take the daisy or ivy stalk to a red rose, an orange tiger lily, a buttercup, the grass, a bluebell an indigo iris and tiny violet.

The colours of these plants all flowed into the daisy or ivy stalk so that the Writshtar would have a never-ending supply of ink in their pen. As the Fae adore all colours, the rainbow narrows down the choice.

Further, the Fae scribe and the pen were together forever. The Writshtar never allows anyone to borrow their pen and no fairy would, as to ask to borrow one's pen is terribly rude and goes against all forms of social acceptability in Faery world.

Divine Writing

To the Fae writing is a gift of the gods as it forms a part of the sacred triangle of truth.

Reading   Writing

Knowledge

The sacred triangle of truth forms the basis of fairy belief and lore. Although the Fae are free to do what they want there is an order to freedom in which they all must adhere to.

Occasionally a rogue fairy will break all convention but they will be taken to the Royal court for questioning. The one rule of the Fae that can never be broken is fairies must never show humans their true appearance.

Many fairies are able to shape shift and appear in human form but if a fairy should appear in their true fairy form then this is a crime and they will be severely punished.

Nevertheless, writing was viewed with great respect in Fay. In ancient Egyptian, the name for hieroglyphs was 'divine speech', such was the respect for writing. Words were believed to be very powerful and of course especially potent in magic and ritual.

The word Hieroglyph is derived from Greek as most of our human words are. Hieroglyph is made from two words in fact, which mean sacred and engrave so literally Hieroglyph means sacred engraved, or translated into 'sacred writing'. Therefore, for the purpose of our study into Fae, the word Faeroglyphs means fairy writing, or fairy engraved, or fairy carved.

All of the symbols used in Fae are derived from nature in

some form to the Fey. As we have already learnt nature is fundamental to the Fey it is what they live and breathe for.

Therefore, any form of writing or any Faeroglyphs, even a name as the pictures of nature depict, all stem from the earth and therefore should be revered.

All writing is sacred and divine just as nature is.

To the Fey, forms of writing could even come to life. The words held such power, and magic was, and is used constantly in everyday life, that on occasion words did come to life and literally jumped off the page and skipped about. Fairies then would have a job to try and catch these runaway words and slap them back onto the page or scroll.

What Fey Wrote

In the beginning the Fey wrote about the reign of their monarchs and their magical ages. Later, they began to write down spells, rituals, magical recipes, songs, rhymes, names and even shopping lists.

The Fey also wrote down stories and plays as faeries adore entertainment, especially theatre. Any excuse to shape shift is a desirable outcome for anything and at any time in life.

One of the most famous actors in Fay is Sir Robin Goodfellow who was created a knight by her Serene Majesty Queen Lily in the later stages of the 4th dynasty.

Sir Robin Goodfellow's true appearance is rare but his other guises such as pixie, hobgoblin, human, crow, or moth leaves Fae mesmerized.

In his true form, Sir Robin has bright white hair is very tall for a fairy, and has striking purple eyes. However, in all his shape shifting forms there is a hint of purple lurking somewhere which reveals his true identity. So, if you happen to see a moth with purple shapes on, or a shiny black crow whose feathers shine iridescent shades of purple in the sun, then you are likely seeing Sir Robin Goodfellow, and should bow your head in respect.

Many of the Fae texts are descriptions of flowers and trees. Then around these natural plants there is a whole host of recipes, spells, uses and descriptions of when the best time to pick the flower and the best season to use the flowers in.

There are also lengthy descriptions of the clothes that faeries wear and who designs them, and of course what materials were used in making them.

Further, there are lengthy biographies of the Royal houses in each age or era, or aeon. At present, we are in the 5th Age which is the Age of Selkie. Fairy children who are born in this age have wings that are blue. This Age of Selkie also sees a rise in the Mer people population including Selkies and Nereids.

How do Faeroglyphs Work?

Alphabet/Faebet

We are now going to begin our study into the actual Faebet. You could try drawing these letters out in your own field study book to acquaint yourself of the signs and symbols you may find out and about.

Further, the reader must excuse my drawings of the Faebet as these are the actual artwork from my field study book. Also, a one word description accompanies some of the pictures, to help the reader understand better how the Fae comes to these ideas.

Fairy Image	Name	Meaning	Letter	Sound
⠇⠄ /⫫\	Arwen	Creativity Inspiration	A	a
⊢	Beith Beth	Beginning Cleansing	B	b
☼	Solaron	Circle of life	C	ck
⊣	Duir	Strength Courage	D	d
∼∼∼	EE	Sea	E	eee
⊬	Fehu	Wealth Luck/Money	F	ff
⊣	Huath	Obstacles Boundaries Fear	H	hhh

Fairy Image	Name	Meaning	Letter	Sound
	Yey (Window)	Look/Sight Truth	I	i as in eye
	Jubber (Adder)	Lies Dishonest	J	jj
	Fut	Games Play	K	kk as in kick,
	Ella (Shell)	Together Friends Family	L	ll
	Muin (Bramble)	Harvest Celebration Happy	M	mmm
	Ning-Nang (Wings)	Freedom Seasons	N	n as in NO!

Fairy Image	Name	Meaning	Letter	Sound
Ω	Ogg (Omega)	The end Final/Last	O	o as in orange
(Lips)	Pippy (Lips)	Skipping Hopping Animals Insects	P	pp
(Apple)	Quert (Apple)	Healing Renewal Avalon Fae	Q	Qu as in Queen
(Stone with a hole)	Pock (Stone with a hole)	Magic Spells Wand	R	r as in rock
(Willow)	Saille (Willow)	Moon Intuition Flexibility	S	sss

Fairy Image	Name	Meaning	Letter	Sound
	Tock (Heart)	Sweets Full Complete	T	tt
	Ur (Heather)	Lovers Partnership Honey Food	U	u as in jug
	Vish (Star)	Wishes Dreams Stardust	V	v as in vain
	Row (Arrow)	Travel Movement Flying/Wings	W	w as in window
	Xai (Snail Shell)	Sleep/Relax Patience	X	X as in X-ray
	Try Triquetra	Connection Balance	Y	Y as in yo-yo
	Ziara (Crown)	Law Authority Rulership	Z	zzzz

Biliterals Phonics

Discriminate, spell, and read the common spelling patterns for long vowel phonemes:

ee (feet), ea (seat), ai (train), ay (play), ie (lie), y (fly)
oa (boat), o-e (pole), ow (show), oo (moon),
ew (flew), ue (blue), oy (toy), ou (sound), ar (car),
oi (boil), er (her, were), ir (bird), aw (claw),
au (caught).

Fairy Image	Name	Meaning	Letter	Sound
Z	Bo (Letter Z)	Lost in the human world	ee	feet
	Mat (Floor plan)	Any rooms in a fairy house	ea	seat
	Casah (Wand)	Career Jobs	ai	train
	Lala (Complete Circle)	Love Eternity	ay	play
	Nop (1 wave)	Liar Amazement	ie	lie
	Sh (Fish)	Sea/Water	oa	boat
	Pit (Hat)	Noble Winner	o-e	pole

Fairy Image	Name	Meaning	Letter	Sound
	Top (Circle with a line)	Completion No more Empty	ow	show
	Shbap (Crescent moon)	Years/Time	oo	moon
	Chuah (Witch's Broom)	Friend/Allie Protector	ew	flew
	Tchar (Feather)	Rainbow Clouds	ue	blue
	Rid (Mirror)	Vanity Beauty	oy	toy
	Das (Cup/Mug)	Meal/Food	ou	sound
	Yip (Pine Tree)	Christmas Midwinter	ar	car

Fairy Image	Name	Meaning	Letter	Sound
～◯～	Yap (Sun with waves)	Midsummer Litha	oi	boil
△ △	Slee (Two triangles balancing)	Vernal Equinox Ostara	er	her
▽ ▽	Nap (Upside triangles)	Autumn Equinox Samhain	ir	Bird
⚘	Mph (Human Shape)	People	au	caught
🍃	Noc (Leaf)	Forgiveness	aw	claw

Triliterals

> *Igh (high), air (fair), are (scare), ere (there),*
> *ear (bear), ore (more), shr (mushroom),*
> *scr (scream), thr (three), spr (spring),*
> *spl (splodge), squ (square), ing (ping).*

Fairy Image	Name	Meaning	Letter	Sound
	Kia (Kite)	Day	igh	high
	Click (Five pointed star)	Night	air	fair
	Shmo (Paw print)	Small animals	are	scare
	Cor (Mountains)	Earth World	ere	there
	Han (Two horns)	Herne the Hunter	ear	bear
	Blip (Three lines to the right)	Future	ore	more

Fairy Image	Name	Meaning	Letter	Sound
	Blap (Three lines to the left)	Past	shr	mushroom
	Zing (Bubbles)	Happy Music Singing	scr	scream
	Fin (Rainbow)	Colours	thr	three
	Dock (Fan)	Lawbreaker	spr	spring
	Posh (Mushroom, toadstool	Dress-maker	spl	splodge
	Tin (Birds flying)	Theatre, Freedom	squ	square
	Floss (Horseshoe)	Racing, sports	ing	ping

The Way to Read Faeroglyphs

There are many ways to read, lots of different people from many different countries, all read differently.

The English read and write horizontally, from left to right. Whilst in China writing is in vertical columns from top to bottom. Text written in Chinese uses little or no punctuation at all. Similar to ancient Egyptian Hieroglyphs, Fae can be read horizontally in two directions: either from left to right or from right to left.

However, there were some scribes in the past ages who began writing from top to bottom and bottom to top. Thankfully, the Monarchs of the Age of Dragon put an end to this heretical style of writing.

Nevertheless, the direction of writing and reading in both horizontal lines and vertical columns of Faeroglyphs depend upon the Age in which the Faeroglyphs stemmed from.

Further, due to this flexibility, faery scribes could compose their writing artistically, especially when it accompanied other pictures such as those of famous Fae or gods, or members of the Royal Households.

The writing would often face the same way as if two fairies sat opposite each other in discussion. Further, if two Fae sat or flew in complete opposite directions, i.e. back to back, then the writing could be divided in the same painting into two groups facing two different ways.

The method of deciding which way Faeroglyphs should be read is to work out the direction they are facing. For example, the Faeroglyphs of Duir, meaning strength and courage and Huath, obstacles and fear, (see Figure 1), all face left so the writing is read left to right.

However, Beth or beginning, and Fehr, meaning wealth and money, are both facing right, therefore, the writing is read right to left.

Linear Faeroglyphs were written in column and are usually only for Royal names and gods. The signs in an individual column can be read starting at the top and working down to the bottom.

Most Faeroglyphs were not written in an exact horizontal line or vertical column but were arranged in small groups. Basically, when it comes to fairy language, anything goes.

Fairies have a rather short attention span also they can be easily angered. Therefore, if a fairy scribe was challenged by an elder or member of the Royal court then their anger and frustration would be taken out on their writing. The Faeroglyph itself would become an obscure image and its true meaning was known only to its scribe.

However, as most fairies did not read the Faeroglyph in question was later looked upon as a work of art. Writing was admired and those who could write were held in high esteem.

Pronunciation

Fae is a strange language. The written language survives but human beings cannot be certain how the language was spoken. The main reason for this are of course physical and spiritual.

We human beings are much bigger than a fairy, and whilst our ears are considerably bigger than a fairy, we still cannot hear fairy language.

Further, fairies generally live within the spiritual dimensions that humans are not permitted to go unless invited by one of the Fey themselves. Therefore, we are unsure as to how precisely to pronounce the words.

When humans do hear the Fey however, we immediately think of the bells tinkling, tiny bells at that. Moreover, when working in woods, or parks and we hear a scratching sound, or knocking sound we immediately think it is a bird or squirrel, or some other form of wild life, when in fact it is a fairy.

Further, ticking sound are also part of the Fae vocabulary. Therefore, we have now identified three sounds of pronunciation of Fae; tinkling, ticking, and knocking, or a ticking-tocking, knock with a rattling and a scratching.

The language of Fay is thousands and thousands of years old and with each new Age a new dialect can come along with new Royal decrees and rules. Each new Age brought with it an emphasis on pronunciation.

The Age of Unicorn for example, brought about the tinkling of bells sound, whilst the Age of Dragon brought about the scratching, rattling sound we hear today.

One of the most common problems we have today as humans trying to learn Fae is the fact that Fey do not write in vowels to create a word the way we do. We know the vowels a, e, i, o, u, when we are learning to read. Further, we know the way these vowels sound and we have rhymes to help us remember their sound and preference. For example:

"When two vowels go out walking it's the   first one that does the talking."

However, not all the time, but it definitely helps to remember that rhyme.

Incidentally, it was a fairy who invented that rhyme when he was trying to learn our language in the human year of 1803. His name was Archibald Archimedes or Archie Arkie to his friends and you can see in his very name the problems with pronunciation and sounds. The Arch in Archibald is pronounced 'ch' whereas the Arch in Archimedes is pronounced 'ark'.

Language and pronunciation is extremely complex but we must learn it in order to do all the wonderful things we do and ultimately to communicate with one another. We all need to communicate with one another, but if only we could find a common language.

Plurals

In English, the most common way to make a plural is to add on an 's' to a word, or noun, therefore, dog becomes dogs. The Fey express plurals in their language either by writing a lot of something. For example, the sign for Queen Daisy Avalon is:

When writing about her children, the scribes would write:

Further, if they wished to indicate a plural on an object they would simply write dots like our O; oooooo, the more dots something has the more important it is, or higher the value.

One of the oldest methods of writing a plural was write three times. Three is a very sacred number and three times a charm. We shall look more at the importance of numbers in the next chapter.

Nevertheless, if for example fairy scribes wished to write stream it would be one wave;

A river is two waves;

The sea is three waves while, a waterfall is;

And somewhere like Niagara Falls is;

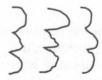

So, the importance and plural of something in Fae is determined by the picture.

The Fey also has a number of ways of showing pairs of things. The most important pair in Fay is of course wings, otherwise known as Ning Nang. While another way of showing, a pair is by cockle shells.

Numbers

Pictograms

Faeroglyphic numbers are very easy to understand. The Fey use a pentacle system of counting with ones, fives, hundreds, and so on.

In English, ten numerals are used e.g. 0, 1, 2, 3, 4, 5, 6, 7, 8, 9, but in Fae only two are used. The reader is then left to do the maths as it were, to work out exactly the sum of faery scribes were writing.

In Fae numbers were usually written with their corresponding symbol, (as in 5, 25), not in words, as in five, twenty-five. In Fae, the two basic numerals were used to cover single units, tens, hundreds, thousands, ten thousand and hundred thousand. There was no sign for zero in Fae as there is no need to write it or show it for if something is nothing then it is nothing and no reason to write nothing.

The basic numbers are:

1 Wa	n Tick 100
x Na	Tock 1000
xx Nana 10 O	Pick 10,000
	Pock 100,000

The sign for one hundred is a bridge, sometimes depicted with a troll underneath it. While the sign for 1000 is a tadpole and for 10,000 is a crop circle, whom the fairies particularly like. The circle does appear time and time again in Fae and one must differentiate whether the image pertaining to a Royal name or Age, or it is a Fairy sum for young fairies to learn counting with.

Therefore, in this respect when reading Faeroglyphs where a circle is found one must look at the bigger picture so to speak and see the meaning within all the signs that accompany it.

The sign of 100,000 or one hundred thousand it pock which does look similar to a pyramid but it is a triangle which is another favourite faery shape.

Any number can be constructed by combining and/or repeating one or more of the basic numbers. A Faeroglyphic number is read simply by adding up what the signs represent. For example, lll is 3, xlll is 8, three hundred is llln.

A Little More Grammar, Vowels, and Consonants

Some elements of the Fae grammar and style of writing has already been addressed. However, anyone intending to make a serious study of Faeroglyphs should learn all the elements of grammar.

Fortunately, Fae has actually very little grammar, for example, Fae sentences do no always have verbs, in fact, Fae rarely has sentences. In the fairy realm sentences and verbs are not that important but it is the meaning of a picture that speaks to Fey. A picture paints a thousand words and a Faeroglyph certainly does that.

Nevertheless, verbs only became important to Fae when Faeroglyphs are translated into English. For example, the two words, 'tree, tall', would be translated into English as, 'the tree is tall'.

Verbs in English have various forms that determine the meaning of the sentence such as, writes, wrote, writing, written. Yet verbs in Fae are not complex they do not exist and neither do nouns for that matter.

Further, as for past, and present participle does not exist as everything Fey do is in the moment. There is no word in their vocabulary for past or future, only the Royal families of history, or the Royalty of tomorrow. Today they know who will be the next King and Queen, but as for fairies making plans, nothing is further from their minds. The Fae believe if something is going to happen then it's going to happen so why bother planning for it?

The Fey are only concerned with the moment and therefore, 'doing' words are a concept that is far beyond the Fey. The Fey do not 'do' anything they simply are!

However, the one piece of grammar Fey scribes do adhere to are adjectives for they love to describe their Royals, their Ages, magic, and especially wings.

So, many beautiful images are designed and written on trees, peoples, rocks, and sacred sites around the world concerning wings. The Fey love clothes, shoes, and caked and these are also described in very, very eloquent adjectives.

Another piece of grammar advice is that Fey do not have masculine or feminine words or pictures as everyone is the same and therefore there are no pronouns such as her, him, my or that.

Your Name

As Faeroglyphs look so very different from all styles of writing it can be fascinating to write your own name and those of friends in Faeroglyphs.

Therefore, when writing English words into Faeroglyphs, the following translations of English sounds into Faeroglyphs are the ones most commonly used.

Use the Faebet as a guide to writing your name. Furthermore, there is no difference in Faeroglyphs between uppercase letters or capitals, (A, B), and lower case letters, (a, b).

Further, if a name does look right in Faeroglyphs then alternations can be tried, because as we know there is often more ways to spell a certain name. Further, as previously stated, when it comes to Fae, anything goes.

Also, names can be made more important by putting a

Faetouche round them, which is bit like a Cartouche, which is an oval shape.

A Faetouche is still an oval shape, but which has also lots of daisies or stars round it. Therefore, because the Fae used Faetouche for the names of Royalty, why not use it also for you.

Here are some names that could be written in Faeroglyphs but any other name can be written using the Faebet found earlier in the book. Also, many of these names can be found in the next chapter, as quite a considerable amount of these names found their way into the Royal Households

Human and Fae names:

AaronAbigail	DawnDeborah
AbelAbraham	DenisDiana
AdabelleAdam	DouglasEdie
AlaricAlexandra	EdwardElijah
AliceAmber	ElizabethElla
AmandaAmelia	ElsieEmanuel
AmyAnastasia	EmilyErwin
AndrewAngharad	EstherEvan
AprilArthur	EvelynEzra
Arwyn/ArwenAva	FairleyFenton
BaileyBeau	FernFindley
BeatriceBenjamin	FloraFlynn
BethanyBilly	FrancisFreya
BlossomBridget	GabriellaGabriel
BrookeCaleb	GaiaGawain
CareryCarwyn	GeorgeGypsy
CecilyChanel	GodivaGodwin
CharlieCharlotte	GradyGresham
ChloeChristabel	GwynethHalliwell
ChristopherCleo	HamarHannah
CodyCraig	HardenHarold
CranleyDaisy	HarrietHarry
DaleyDanae	HeatherHelen
DanielDavid	HenryHoratio

HunterHuxley
IainIgnatius
Imogen Isaac
IsabellaIsla
IvyJacintha
JacobJack
JacquelineJames
JasminJennifer
JeremyJessica
JonahJosiah
JoyceJulietta
KatherineKay
KentonKieran
KristinaKyle
LaceyLancelot
LawrenceLeah
LeightonLily
LincolnLogan
LukeLucy
LyndonMadelaine
MadisonMarcus
MarianneMarlene
MarlowMaximillian
MelodyMichael
MilfordMonroe
MontyNatalya
NessaNewlyn
NicholasNoah
NualaOakley
OdetteOlivia
OlivierOriel
OrlandoOswin
OstarOwen
OzziePaige
PatiencePabruck
PearlPenelope
PerditaPerry

PeterPhoebe
PiperPoppy
PrudenceQuentin
QuintusQuinn
RachelRafe
RanulphRaphael
RawleyRiley
RheiaRhiannon
RidleyRoald
RobertRosemary
RowanRufus
RussellRylan
SadieSally
SamuelSarah
ScarlettScott
SeeleySiwald
ShanleySheridan
SophieStella
SukieSutton
TabithaTalitha
TennysonThaddeus
TheoThomas
TireeToby
ToriTrahene
TravisTrent
TrudieTyler
UlmerUriel
Ursula Valentina
VanceVivien
WadeWallis
WebsterWendy
WhitleyWinston
WoodrowWinnifred
WilliamXavier
XeniaYale
YasminYork
ZacharyZara
ZinniaZoe

Time Line of Fae Ages

There are many who believe our human world is older than first thought. However, for the Fae this has always been the case. They have always believed that human historians got things wrong but then again, the Fae have always thought humans get everything wrong!

The world, our earth, is said to be 4.5 billion years old, so it has been here quite a while. Further, our human ancestors have been here for about six million years. Although the modern humans evolved about 200,000 years ago. Yet what about fairies?

This amazing world we live in keeps evolving and so do we, though changes take thousands of years. Fairies have evolved alongside humans, though in some form magic has been with the earth since its very inception. Fairies too have been here for roughly 250,000 years, possibly longer as we have very little to go on. Remember, the first Writshtars were not commissioned until the Age of Unicorn.

The very first Age, the Age of Avalonia is just a mystery to us as it is to our fellow friends, the Fae. However, what we do know is that most of the ancient spells and rituals stem from the Age of Avalonia as fairy priest and priestesses used to pass everything orally.

Though in fairy language orally meant 'wingly'. As the very first fairies spoke only with their wings.

The very first Age was the Age of Avalonia and it truly was the beginning. The mythical King Thornang and Queen Bethning created a dynasty of peace and wonder.

We say mythical as the King performed such great fetes of magic and wonder that no fairy could have been that powerful, but maybe he was? He was said to have commanded the stars of the heavens to show themselves and to speak louder so much so the night sky would tinkle with the sound of twinkling stars.

It was said that fairies would dance all night to the sounds of heaven. He also told the moon to come down and bathe herself in the sea, as she was dirty from all the dust in space. As the moon did she shook herself dry and all the drops of water mingles with moon magic and as they fell back into the water, the Mer people were created.

The Age of Avalonia is looked upon as a beautiful age full of wonderment, peace and joy. Some young fairies of today look back at that age and try to recreate the carefree, and happier existence of Avalonians. However, as fairies they do dream and think of many strange things.

The Age of Avalonia was a time before time. The Aborigine people of Australia described it best when they called it, The Dreaming. A time of such magic and mystery that anything was possible. So much so that no particular element governed this Age.

In Fae time, as beings of nature, each Age is governed by an element which pre-determines the kind of fairies being born to that Age.

The five elements for humans, are; earth, air, fire, water, and Spirit or divinity. The five elements for fairies are; earth, air, fire, water, and the Universal Matrix. A concept that we shall study further in the Gods and Goddesses Chapter.

However, in this Age, the Age of Avalonia, the Universal Matrix was simply, the beginning. The beginning of all magical life as we know it. A time when pixies, Elves, and the Mer people came into being. The race that crowned this time was the Fae.

After about 50,000 years the next Age that came into being was the Age of Unicorn which was governed by the element of earth.

It was said the Age of Unicorn was truly magical, as this was the Age of the golden bluebell. These exquisite flowers are no longer to be found in the wild or anywhere as they are now quite extinct. Though perhaps this has something to do with how magical their properties were, and both Royalty and witches alike picked and used these plants until they were no more.

It was due to this extinction that a decree was made by the then ruling monarch, that all plants and flowers be given special protection, and so wood nymphs became the guardians of nature. The decree also made sure that both witches and Monarchs have a special licence to use the powerful properties of plants.

The Age of Unicorn saw the rise of Leprechauns, Gnomes, Elves of the woods and forests, not to mention the nymphs, and the Green Man. Further, the Age of Unicorn saw the birth of giants, trolls and ogres.

The Fae that were born at this time had green wings. These Fae were very practical and down to earth, that is probably why we find writing being developed in this Age. The Fae of this Age were rather discipline for fairies and everything was extremely methodical. We can still glimpse their magnificent monuments across the land with the white horses of the South Downs.

The Age of Unicorn also saw the alliance between the natural world and the magical one. Animals and insects worked alongside to bring about harmony, almost a symphony of sounds that drew upon the interconnectedness of all.

However, this synergy of togetherness was almost destroyed with the arrival of the next two ages. As the Age that followed the Unicorn was the Age of Griffin.

This Age was governed by Air, so the elementals of Air took precedence over everything. Air is something that we do not see but need to survive just like magic itself. Air is invisible and this gave rise to the magical world becoming invisible.

Fae, Elves, Pixies, Mer people, Nymphs, Giants, Trolls, and Ogres all could manifest the magic of the Age and its element, and therefore, become invisible, and a great many did. As it is at this time also we see the involvement of the human world which encroached onto the magical kingdom.

It was deemed safer to be invisible to human eyes, by the ruling Monarchs, as so many Fae and other elementals has been captured by humans and used in spells and fairy tales.

It is worth a note here also concerning the Ages, for not only was each governed by an element but they were also overseen by the deities of that element. Therefore, in the Age of Griffin, for example the element of Air is governed by Hermes who had wings on his sandals, so he was able to fly here and there, causing mayhem and mischief. However, more shall be said on deities in the next chapter.

In this Age, Queen Leanna ruled in the first dynasty and hers was a great moment in Fae history as she brought with her creative inspiration.

Queen Leanna was known as Leanan Sidhe, pronounced Lanawn Shee, and was a native Irish air sprite. She was highly regarded in artistic circles, especially in the musical world.

The Age of Griffin saw not only the rise of musical and creative accomplishments but also the rise of Griffins, Air Sprites, the Sphinx, and not to mention, the Will o' the Wisp.

However, the Will o' the Wisp is often mistake to be of the element of fire but he truly is one of the air elementals as he appears as a wispy, floating orb of white gas, giving an almost smoky illusion about him.

It was at this time, in the Age of Griffin, that a great many pieces of treasure were buried by Will o' the Wisp. However, it is said that not all the treasure was found and that is why to this day, Humans are still finding buried treasure in their gardens and land. The is because Will o' the Wisps buried everything they could find from gold to pottery, to jewels, and to crowns!

The Fae born in the Age of Griffin has yellow wings which represented the air. Whilst Royalty of this Age always had silver wings.

In the Age of Griffin, there was also a rise in the fairies of the air, in particular, the mist Fae, Tiddy Mun, but we shall visit his story further in the chapter on famous fairies.

The next Age to form on this magical timeline was the Age of Dragon. In the Age of Dragon, we see a rise in some of the most frightening beings of the enchanted realm.

The Age of Dragon, brought about of course, not only a rise in dragons and salamanders, but also the Banshee. An Irish death Spirit who is heard to wail with screams when a true Irish person is about to die. She is said to have fiery red eyes from her weeping but in truth no-one who has seen her, as lived to tell the tale.

It is worth noting further, that the Age of Dragon also saw

the rise of the Djinn or Genie in our world. Though predominately in the Middle East, they found their way to us via humans who travelled on the ancient trade routes. The Djinn could manifest any wishes a mortal could desire but always at a cost. Genies are first and foremost tricksters thus, the need to keep these mischievous elementals at a distance is a must.

The Fae that were born in this Age had red coloured wings whilst Royalty had gold.

The Age we are in now is the Age of the Selkie, and the water element prevails, that is why the human world in this Age is also affected, we either have too little water or too much. We know sea levels are rising and there are many storms which bring flooding. In this Age, we have also seen the rise of tsunamis and these are reminders that we need to live and work in harmony with the natural world.

The Age of Selkie, has seen the rise of not only Selkies of course, but also the Undine, the Mer Folk, and the Gwargedd Annwn, pronounced 'grageth anoon'. She is a Welsh water sprite and is described as very blonde and slender.

We know her as another name and that is The Lady of the Lake. This wonderful being is gentle and king and wishes humans many blessings.

The Naiad and Nereid also prevail in the Age of Selkie. This is a very turbulent time we are living in, giving the nature of the element that rules it.

Fairies and their Gods

Xenophanes said if horses could draw they would draw their gods as horses. As fairies are beings of nature, then their gods are of nature though the concept is very difficult to explain.

Fairies do not have many gods and goddesses they have one god who is both male and female. This god has four masks that change; spring, summer, autumn, and finally, winter.

The fairy god with four masks is very changeable, like Robin Goodfellow and other shapeshifters, but actually just one god who wears masks; the seasons are the masks of God.

Primarily because of the changeable nature of the seasons and weather, god's true appearance would and can also change.

This leads onto the concept of the Universal Matrix, where everything is connected by a silken thread of time and space. It means that we are all connected within this vast universe we live in from humans to Fae to nature. We, therefore, have a responsibility to not only ourselves, but to one another.

Though there is only one god in Fae, there are many legends and myths on how the world came into being. Such as how fairies actually arrived on earth.

Some wise humans have said it was when the first human baby was born. As the baby laughed for the very first time, the laugh broke into a thousand pieces and began to skip about, and this became fairies.

Although the Fae do like this idea, they themselves have ideas about how life began. It is also told by the Fae Priests and Priestess that while the world was being created, the stars had no order and where left to do as they please. So, as stars, they began to have a game of bumping into each other to see who could knock the other down.

However, little did they know that as they bumped into each other, little flecks of dust fell from them and drifted to earth. This is what made fairies. Therefore, fairies are made of stardust, that is why they sparkle the way they do. Moreover, if you ever catch one you are never meant to touch their wings as they are so delicate and fragile, but we shall return later to the importance of fairies and their wings.

Another equally charming creation myth concerns the birth of dragons. The Sun had a sister who said she was faster than him. So, they had a race but crashed into one another, and as they did in a giant explosion, five baby dragons fell to the earth. As a result, the sister Sun lost all her fiery strength and became the moon that we see in the night sky.

As previously mentioned there are other 'deities' that make an appearance throughout Fae lore. However, this is what is referred to as the Hierarchy of the Divine. Though there is one god with four masks, god couldn't be everywhere all the time and so the elements and their guardians were made. We have already seen that Hermes rules Air but what of the other three elements?

Prometheus rules fire, and Cerridwen rules earth, whilst the Lady of the Lake governs waters. These four beings are known as the Ancients and they are the next level from Fae Royalty and the mediators between God and all elementals.

When great decisions need to be made then the Fae counsel is called and the ruling elemental deity sits at the round table. The table is round to represent that, communication continues eternally, even when we run out of things to say, we are still communicating.

Royal Houses

In the five Ages, there have been ruling Monarchs of the Fae kingdom. In each Age a ruling monarchy lasts 10,000 years. The ruling Monarchs' era is called a dynasty. Therefore, if an Age lasts 50,000 years there are five ruling Monarchs, or five dynasties in an Age.

There follows the list of Fae Kings and Queens from each Age.

The Age of Avalonia

First Dynasty

King Thornang and Queen Bethning created a dynasty of peace and wonder.

Second Dynasty

King Tishoo and Queen Hatishoo in the First Age were rather an odd couple, even for fairies. King Tishoo was a bit of an explorer and wandered off the edge of the world.

However, people are now discovering pyramids and faces on the planet Mars, and it is highly likely that King Tishoo found his way to Mars.

Queen Hatishoo was left to rule on her own for the majority of their reign. It is said she was a much better King than her husband could ever be.

Third Dynasty

King Tutnang and Queen Nefnang were all accounts a very

glamourous couple. It is said that theirs was truly a beautiful reign.

Fourth Dynasty

King Tutning and Queen Nefering tried to uphold their predecessors but unfortunately, they lacked the natural grace of King Tutnang and Queen Nefnang.

Fifth Dynasty

King Carerynang and Queen Adabellenang were so unique that it is they became living statues of Fae.

The Age of Unicorn

First Dynasty

King Fairley-Corn and Queen Arwen were very methodical in everything they did but were rather boring to say the least.

Second Dynasty

King Fenton-Bean and Queen Ava began to think of ways to record the history of Fey.

Third Dynasty

King Kenton-Wise and Queen Flora decided to leave a lasting record of their presence. The first Writshtars were appointed by this King and Queen.

Fourth Dynasty

King Leighton-Star and Queen Fern set the very first Faeroglyphic counsel up in this Age of Unicorn.

Fifth Dynasty

King Roald-Beam and Queen Gwyneth-Blossom continued as their predecessors and ensured the succession of Writshtars and continuation of the Faeroglyphic counsel.

The Age of Griffin

First Dynasty

Queen Leanna ruled alone in this Age of Air, and it was said to the most artistic and creative Age ever to have been seen by the Fae.

Second Dynasty

King Erwin and Queen Ursula-Blossom was a descendent of Queen Gwyneth-Blossom, and as such retained some of the Age of Unicorn's disciplined and methodical emphasis.

Third Dynasty

King Oriel and Queen Danae were very astute at keeping

the musical and artistic emphasis alive.

Fourth Dynasty

King Pabruck and Queen Melody made a really beautiful couple. King Pabruck was a Writshtar who found his way up to the highest order in the land due to his superb talents.

Fifth Dynasty

King Emmanuel and Queen Zinnia were the final rulers of the Age of Griffin and ensured that creativity and musical ability would always be first and foremost within the land of Fey.

Age of Dragon

First Dynasty

King Hunter – Wise and Queen Nessa were an extremely powerful couple. Many laws and rules were brought in by this power crazed couple.

Second Dynasty

King Hamar-Storm and his Queen, Winifred-Blossom, who was a descendent to the Fae Blossoms of previous Ages, were a completely different couple compared to their predecessors. Whereas, the previous Dynasty had commanded total obedience, this couple had the attitude of, 'whatever!'

Third Dynasty

King Harden and Queen Trudie were Monarchs who helped humans to build great monuments by flying great dragons of the Age. In order to carry the huge stones from Wales and other places for monuments such as Stonehenge amongst others.

Fourth Dynasty

King Iggy-Crane and Queen Imogen-Tuck, also helped humans create castles and fortresses, including the great vitrified fortresses of Aberdeenshire and other places.

Vitrification is a process whereby stone turns to glass, this is only done by extreme heat, hence, dragon's breath. There are over sixty vitrified forts across Scotland, the amount of fire the dragons must have to produce is simply astounding!

Fifth Dynasty

King Ostar and Queen Amber were a very stunning couple and their portraits can be seen all over the world. Many fairy houses have pictures and paintings of these two simply stunning looking Monarchs hanging in their homes just simply to gaze at and enjoy their beauty.

The Age of Selkie (which we are now in – the first Dynasty)
First Dynasty

King Beau-Wood and Queen Pearl rule today in Fae. They are responsible for ensuring the continuation of their kind and the enchanted realm. As this royal couple are only in the early stages of their 10,000-year reign there is little to be said about it. Although, never before has the enchanted realm and in particular, the Fairy Kingdom, been in so much danger. The threat comes from their neighbours, humans of course, but it will be difficult to say how it will turn out if humans get their way of completely ridding the world of magic. Their constant greed and hatred towards one another destroys the harmonious balance between the worlds. It is a very difficult time we live in.

A Few Famous Fairies

Sir Robin Goodfellow

Actor, Shape Shifter Extraordinaire

This intricate Fae must NOT be trusted in any of his guises. He is often thought of as a goblin or even a demon. He has many names along with his many disguises. He is known as Puck, the Welsh call him Pwca, which is pronounced the same as his Irish incarnation; the Pooka.

In his guise as the Pooka, he can appear as a black hors or large black dog and is known for taking life. In other words, similar to the Banshee, he is a harbinger of death.

Yet despite all his negativity, there is a mesmerising quality about him which draws humans and Fae alike to him.

Tiddy Mun

The Tiddy Mun is an ancient Fae who can curse children, cattle and the elderly for crossing him.

Tiddy Mun is the King of the Tiddy, a race of Fae that could control the tide, and waters of the marshes of East Anglia, in particular Lincolnshire.

The Tiddy were a race of pixie people who lived in the wetlands. They were inherently neither good nor evil; if you helped them they would reward you, cross them then beware.

Human interference proved the later when in the seventeenth century, people drained the marshes. A curse fell on the children, cattle, and the elderly, with many dying.

In the end Tiddy Mun lifted the curse after humans began to pour water back onto the land.

He is often said to appear as a grey mist over the land. People sometimes refer to Tiddy Mun as the fog fairy or a weather fairy, but he is considerably more dangerous than this and should not be taken lightly.

Time and Seasons

In the world of Fae, time is eternal and cyclical. When a being lives for almost 10,000 years, time itself can stand still, and this is just one of the many magical secrets of the Fae.

In regards to this Fae obviously have no need for watches or clocks as humans would understand. Instead there is a giant clock in the great hall at the heart of Avalonia. The clock which is decorated so exquisitely, tells the Ages and includes the Royal Dynasties attached to them. It truly is a remarkable piece of engineering, and one in which, not many humans have seen.

Yet this division between humans and Fae is blurred when it comes to the seasons, as both human and Fae alike, are all affected by the natural world and its seasons.

The seasons for the Fae are marked, in particular, by the Festivals themselves. For example, in the month what humans would call June, the Fae call it, Litha, after the festival, which is of course, Midsummer.

Here is a list of the Fae months and in particular the corresponding seasons and festivals. The Human months are in brackets.

Samhain (October-December)

Samhain is the beginning of a new year, although this occurs in the months October/November for humans, this is the most magical time of the year for Fae.

The actual festival or New Years' Day is Samhain and humans view this as Halloween, a mixture of scary and silly. It is silly but many Fae love it as it is a time to dress up and attend one of the many Samhain Masquerade Balls which are held at this time of year. Great feasting, fun, and frivolity of all kinds are experienced with the main colours being orange and black, many Fae turn up with tiger masks.

Samhain also sees many Will O' Wisps' look for treasure. The Tiddy Mun also make an appearance at this time of year. The Fog Fae are out in their droves across the Moors and Wolds of Lincolnshire and Yorkshire, with many a naïve wanderer being in lost in their mysterious charms.

Yule (December – January)

This is another wonderful time of the Fae year for merry making and having in fun. In fact, the Fae's year is full of opportunities to have parties which include lots of singing and dancing. One might say that, that is all a Fae year consists of; one giant party. Though it is true that Fae are very sociable beings and love meeting friends, playing dress up, having a Ball or several, but they can be serious too, although very few times. As when a fairy does become rather serious their wings tend to fade, which we will look into further the importance of wings in the next chapter.

Nevertheless, returning to Yule, this is a charming part of the year with winter well and truly under way. The large red berries on holly and hawthorn give sway to the evergreens and ivy that grows in abundance at this time of year.

There are many winter Balls with sumptuous meals, stout hearty broths, and flowing acorn cups full of brandy wine and heather beer.

The festival they celebrate is Yule and similar to the human variety of Yule they celebrate the return of the King. As traditionally the Fae King, from the new year till now, has been travelling the enchanted realm attending meetings and negotiating trade for the forthcoming year.

Also, in the time of Yule, many baby dragons are born, some believe this is due to all the roaring fires that are abound. Further, the Fae are particularly fond of the poem Twas the Night Before Yule and often recite it the night before the actual festivities begin.

Imbolc (February- Beginning of March)

This is one of the most charming times of the year and one in which, the Fae absolutely adore. Imbolc is the season which brings the first signs of spring. In human terms, it is the months of February and March.

The Fae are eager for this time of year as clothes are changed from winter to spring colours, and all Fae love green. The green that appears at this time of year is never seen again throughout the rest of the year. It is the fresh, young, spring green, which is almost a light, lime refreshing colour. The fairies love nothing more than flying past a spring hedgerow gathering all the different greens available.

This season brings the Fae fashion designers out and many new clothes of future seasons are exhibited. In fact, this time of year is the fashion extravaganza of the Fae world. Royalty and Fae from all corners of the globe descend on Avalonia, with many cultures and races all enjoying the season with harmony and love.

The fashion parties are filled with beautiful foods of delicate spring flowers; crocus drops, snowdrop cake, and hyacinth wine, not to mention the delicious Cawl, and Bara brith, or speckled bread.

The first races are held, amongst them the Catkins Derby. All Fae are out in force for this day, wearing their finest spring attire. It is a sight to behold.

Ostara (End of March- Beginning of April)

The Fae often refer to this as the yellow month due to the daffodils, jonquils, and yellow aconites that are out. The Fey towns and cities are awash with the colours of green, white and yellow with this festival.

Many Fae are wearing their spring greens whilst rebellious young ones are wearing daffodil yellows and the young Writshtars, those who are new to their profession, wear white. As Writshtars, every respect is given to them as they go about their daily chores. They are served first in shops, and Fae Food Spas. The Fae do not have restaurants in the human sense of the term, instead they have a food spa.

The idea of somewhere to eat and then leave within a couple of hours is completely unknown in Fey. The process of eating is a very special, social and joyous thing therefore, a food spa, is where Fey go to spend all day eating, drinking, and being indulged.

Ostara is also the traditional time of the year when Leprechauns, Brownies, and hobgoblins are born.

Beltane (End of April – May)

This is a marvellous season and with it comes so much colour. The rainbow Fae are out in force from the April showers, and the May flowers are brought forth, giving an abundance of colour explosions within the natural world. The Fae literally paint the whole world with colour at this time; red, yellows, blues, greens, purples, oranges, every colour imaginable can be in the May garden.

The festival itself is Beltane and it is regarded as the fire festival of spring. Many salamanders are born at this time, along with a number of pixies, and of course flower fairies, and their counterpart fire fairies, which are not often spoken off.

There are also magnificent spring Balls for this season and its glorious flowers. The Balls of this season are the magnificent masquerade Ball of the King and Queen who dress with all the finery that the season brings. Fantastic foods, glistening with May dew give a diamond shine to everything. If ever there was a feast that looked truly magical then the spread for the Beltane Masquerade Ball held at the Palace of Dreams is the one. It is said no human has ever seen witnessed, it is only recorded by the Writshtars on court documents that humans come to understand and know of it.

At the Ball, there is also a Maypole which young Fae use to fly round, looping the ribbons with time and space.

Litha (June-July)

The wonderful season of Litha or Midsummer, as humans call it, is the pinnacle of the year. There is so much to see, do, eat, drink and generally, have as much fun as fairy possible.

There are wonderful Midsummer Balls all over the kingdom and Fae and troll alike all partake in Midsummer Punch. This is a special beverage made with the flowers, and nectar of the peach blossoms of the previous months. It is very potent and even the smallest amount can send an average ogre into a deep sleep. So, it is recommended that only one small acorn cup can be used by the average fairy for this intoxicating drink.

Many games, races, and fashion shows happen now during this season, along with Fae marriages. Indeed, the present King and Queen celebrated their four thousandth, wedding anniversary on a Midsummer in the human year of 1724.

Litha is a season to enjoy life, friends, family, and food, and usually altogether.

This is also a season when most the baby Fae are born, though in the Age of Selkie, many Mer Folk have also been born. The baby Fae of this Age are quite extraordinary looking, they are even more beautiful than the average fairy. They have big beautiful blue eyes and exquisite blue wings that make a 'shoosing' sound like the sea.

Lammas (August)

This is a rather melancholy season for the Fae as even though it is in the height of the summer for humans, there is a change in the air. The highly sensitive Fae can sense this and this season is the only time when a fairy can get sick. So, fairy doctors are usually very busy at this time of year, making sure all their patients are healthy and happy and enjoying all the good things the world can give.

At this season, lots of bread and in particular Bara brith is made and in typical Fae fashion this time of year, a special time of Bara brith is made; a sugar coated one. All this lovely fresh bread is washed down with plenty of honey wine, which is often mistaken to be mead but the two are completely different, just ask any weary traveller from the human world, who is foolish to drink any, or eat any of the speckled bread.

There are many parties of course and many pixies at this time of year celebrate Lammas with making their own form of Bara brith, which is called Lammas bread. Many pixie households have their own traditional recipe for Lammas bread but all include honey, and sunflowers in some quantity.

Mabon (September)

Mabon is a beautiful season, and is the second harvest festival of the year with Lammas being the first, hence the bread making.

Mabon, is a sumptuous festival of the orchard harvest with apples, pears, plums, and peaches all in abundance.

The harvest festivals and parties of the Fae go on for basically the entire month of September. Many games, sports, racing, and fashion parades take place in the cities across the enchanted realm now, as the fruits of the earth are shown off and welcomed.

It is also a time when the first mushrooms begin to make an appearance in the woods and forests, much to the fairies' delight. Many a good mushroom has found its way into a fairy's house to be used new furniture for the coming winter. That is generally what fairies do, they never really redecorate their houses they just have new furniture which is usually made from nature in some way, so in fairness it will need changing from year to year.

The festival of Mabon coincides with the Autumnal Equinox when both day is equal to night, and is a very auspicious and magical time. There is a prophecy that a twice blessed child will make their appearance on this day, and they will bring about a new dawn of awareness between the Fae and humans. Though no-one really knows for sure when this babe will be born which is usually the case with prophecy.

These seasons and festivals we have looked at are a remarkable window into the world of the Fae. Yet, there is a wonderful coincidence about them as many humans are now beginning to follow these very same festivals. The witches have always followed them, but many other traditions embraced these certain times of the year. Ostara, for example, which falls around the time of the Vernal equinox or spring equinox, found its way and crossed over into Christianity to become Eostre or Easter. A time of renewal and rebirth, and resurrection.

Whilst, Lammas has also been embraced as harvest festival, with bread being a part of the Christian service, giving thanks to nature. The Fae were very pleased when they found out that, as they always thought humans did not care about the nature and the environment, but in some small corners of the world there are pockets of change. It is these small, wonderful pockets of change that need to be nurtured and perhaps they will begin to pollinate other parts of the world with positive change for all who live within this earth. As that is how the Fae think, that good thoughts and deeds are like seeds of a flower, which need to be nurtured and then when the time is right the seeds fly off to seek other places to grow.

It is worth remembering that another name for fairies, are, the People of Peace.

Body and Wings

We have discussed a number of stereotypes throughout this book and hopefully have realised how important wings are to fairies.

We have discussed how in each Age, fairies are born with the corresponding colour of wings; blue for the Age of Selkie, red for the Age of Dragon, green for the Age of Unicorn, and yellow for the Age of Griffin.

We also know now that fairies whose wings are gold or silver are Fae Royalty. Some houses do have royal Fae babies but sometimes when there is a special need Royal Fae babies will be born into the average everyday Fae families, much to their pleasure. Imagine, magic brings you a Royal Fae to raise and then one day take to the palace to be presented to the ruling Monarchs. These very special Fae and their families are treated like Royalty from then on.

The Blossoms of the past Ages were like that. They were not born of Royalty but born of normal Fae parents but with golden wings. In many ways, when Royalty is of the Fae they seem so much better at being Kings and Queens, and the rest of enchanted kingdom respects them that bit more.

Another reminder about wings, is that the Fae cannot live without them and cannot go anywhere without them. If a Fae loses their wings they die, or their wings are injured then they are very ill, and a great many Fae Priests, and Priestesses try to help with their magic. However, ultimately, white witches are called upon to help them in these dire situations. As a good witch's magic is very powerful and her knowledge of spells is second only to the Fae themselves, but the white witch is also human and knows of human medicines that may also help. So, by enlisting the help of a good white witch, the Fae are getting the best of both worlds.

It is also worth remembering what was stated previously about wings. When a fairy gets sad or serious their wings begin to fade, and a fairy cannot fly if their wings begin to lose their sparkle.

Fae can only fly when their wings are bright, shiny, and buzzing with happy thoughts and laughter.

In fact, their wings do generally emit a low buzzing noise like a bee's, but much fainter. This buzzing is the secret as to why and how fairies can fly, this noise lifts them off and they are able to zoom and dart here and there.

Although, not all fairies do use their wings for travel as some such as Irish fairies prefer to ride the blades of grass like horses that bob up and down, as the grass is blown along by the wind. Though some Irish fairies are very good at uttering magic words and dart here and there on their blades of grass like the witches of the past, on their brooms.

Further, whilst in Ireland let us not forget the Leprechauns and their favourite way to get around, using the rainbow, which also brings them to their favourite possession, their crocks of gold.

However, Leprechauns also love the wild hunt as many Fae do, and on many a night in Ireland, it is often reported that in special counties such Kerry, Galway, and Connemara, little lights can be seen coming down the mountains by Leprechauns riding tiny horses. Incidentally, the South West of Ireland is one of the remaining strongholds of the Fae and it is truly a magical place for any human to visit.

Nevertheless, the importance of wings is paramount to all Fae. Some may not have wings but do not be fooled, all Fae have wings but they can put them away if they chose, and make their wings invisible.

The body of a fairy is also very special and is also blessed with magical powers, especially their legs, which are usually very long and sleek. Their hair, depending on the colour is also very magical and when they shake it, space dust, or as children like to call it, magic dust falls it. Many female fairies have long hair whilst many males will keep their hair short. It is only the Elf male that will have their long hair which they usually braid.

All in all, the body and wings of any fairy is truly magical and if you ever have the chance to see one, try to take a photo of them. Though, I would advise caution as they can be very suspicious of anything technological and will usually instantly disappear or make themselves invisible.

A Few Place Names

There are few human place names that still have the potential of Fae living there. Most of the Wessex triangle is a good place to try to locate them, especially the Vale of the White Horse, or Stonehenge. Cornwall of course is also a hotspot of Fae activity.

In Somerset, there is a place called Glastonbury and whilst it is very busy during the summer months, high on the Tor there is the potential to see the fairies of early morning sunrise, or the evening summer sunset.

In the north of England there are certain pockets of activity believed to be the Fae. One of the famous cases was that of Cottingley, in West Yorkshire. When two cousins photographed the Fae of the Beck in 1917. These photos were published and the good and the great of the day made comments regarding it. However, as previously stated, we know that the Fae do not take kindly to modern technology and will never allow themselves to be photographed.

Nevertheless, this does lead to the final chapter in which we will discuss the presence of fairies in the human world.

However, returning the British Isles, Scotland also has the Fae kingdom, with the magical world taking form in the shape of Nessie, or the Loch Ness Monster, which is such a shame she is called this. The famous Scottish Fae are the Brownies, who are wonderful house Fae who love a tidy and clean house. If you supply them with milk and cheese, they will be forever happy.

Then passing over the Irish Sea to Ireland we find ourselves in the land of the Saints, and although this blessed Isle is full of the Fae legends, many now have retreated to the South West corner. As previously mentioned the Counties of Kerry, Galway, and Connemara have many Fae living amongst its mountains.

The whole of Wales is magical so anywhere in the wonderful country, is possible for seeing the Fae. In this country in particular, by great attention to the weather, especially in the summer, when the mist and rain can rise from the mountains as if lifting a veil, for then is the time that the Fae are descending into the human world.

The Last Word

This little book about the little people, or the 'good neighbours', has been the beginning of a series of books about the Fae. There is so much study and new information being released about the Fae, that their sacred writing is paramount in understanding them.

As the human world begins to close in on itself, there are a few people who look beyond the boundaries of reality and the norm, and what to see what is possible. These people are those that seek answers to the eternal questions regarding our planet and our world we live in.

The existence of the Fae seems to pop up in human history when they are truly needed. Such as in 1917, the height of the First World War, when so much pain and horror was seen in the world. Two little girls in Yorkshire saw the Faery realm and believed.

The same is happening now with the world in chaos once more. When the world truly needs magic, the Fae and their stories return to us to help us see the light in a world grown dark by war and greed.

Therefore, become enlightened, grab your field book and go outside, begin to record everything you see. However, remember, you need to be out in nature and never drink, or eat anything that a strange person gives you, even if they are in human form. You never know, it might even be Sir Robin Goodfellow, and then there would be no way of getting back!

Till we meet again.
R.G.F

Acknowledgments

The editor is indebted to Professor Riley George Fellows for this remarkable piece of work. However, the Professor has been missing for some time, last seen entering a cave somewhere in Wiltshire. We wish him well and a safe return.

The editor would also like to thank Shutterstock for the following images: The Ogham Alphabet, Safety Signs, Crop Circles and Nazca Lines All other illustrations of the Fae writing belong to the Professor.

The editor would also like to thank the writers of The Little Book of Egyptian Hieroglyphs, (2001), Lesley & Roy Atkins, (Hodder & Stoughton) for being a very good, clear book that the Professor enjoyed whilst out in the field.

Ava will return in
The Dragon, The Witch and The Thirteen